A MOTHER'S PRAYER

WRITTEN BY:

NATIONAL BESTSELLING AUTHOR
MZ. BIGGS

Acknowledgments from Mz. Biggs:

These past few months for me have been nothing but a bunch of hurdles seemingly getting in my way to block me from reaching my ultimate goal, which is to succeed in life and show my children than anything is possible. Divorce, heartbreak, the loss of a job, depression, anxiety... you name it, I've been through it. At the end of the day, the only thing I can say is #ButGod. So many times, the thought of giving up hit me hard. Giving up on writing, giving up on love, giving up on life as a whole, but I couldn't. There are not enough words in the vocabulary to express the amount of gratitude I have for the many blessings He's bestowed upon me.

Biggs Publishing Group, LLC is my publishing company and my baby. I'm working hard to brand it and make it be one of the best publishing companies out there. A big shout out to my authors: Author Shawnte Henderson (Author of Envy and King of Hearts in our Valentine's Anthology-A Killer Valentine's), Libra King (Author of Heart for Heart in our Valentine's Anthology-A Killer Valentine's), Dequllarae (Author of Young, Rich, & Savage), Ladi Cooki, and Teea Lynn. The BPG team is working hard to bring you some heat that will leave you begging for more. To my boo, Kianna, whom I've grown to love, your resilience and honesty is indescribable. I'm so glad to have someone like you in the corner of the team. You ROCK!

To my pen sisters, Twyla T. and Margaret Cooper, thanks for having my back. Especially when I have you proofing behind me at the last minute. I love you ladies to the moon and back.

To my readers, both new and old, I appreciate you for taking the time out to read my work. The support means a lot. Feel free to reach out to me via the information below. I do ask that you leave me a review after reading this book. Christian Fiction is a new genre for me, so I'd love to hear your thoughts on this book, whether good or bad. Thank you in advance and Happy Reading...

~Mz. Biggs :-)

Want to connect with me? Here's how:

Email: authoress.mz.biggs@gmail.com

Twitter: **@mz_biggz**

Instagram: **mz.biggs**

Goodreads: **Mz. Biggs**

Facebook: https://www.facebook.com/authoress.biggs

Author Page: https://www.facebook.com/MzBiggs3/

Look for my Reading Group on Facebook: **Lounging With Mz. Biggs**

Check Out These Other Great Books By Mz. Biggs:

See What Had Happened Was: A Contemporary Love Story

(1-3)

Yearning For The Taste of a Bad Boy (1-3)

Dirty South: A Dope Boy Love Story

Falling for A Dope Boy (1-3)

Feenin' For That Thug Lovin (1-3)

Jaxson and Giah: An Undeniable Love (1-2)

Finding My Rib: A Complicated Love Story

In love With My Cuddy Buddy (1-2)

Your Husband's Cheating On Us (1-3)

From Cuddy Buddy To Wifey: Levi and Raven's Story

(Standalone)

In Love With My Father's Boyfriend (Standalone)

Your Husband's Calling Me Wifey (Standalone)

She's Not Just A Snack... She's A Whole Buffet: BBWs Do It

Better (Standalone)

Blood Over Loyalty: A Brother's Betrayal (Standalone)

Married to the Community D (Part 1)

Downgraded: From Wifey to Mistress (1-2)

A Mother's Prayer

Prelude:

Esther

"Come on, Stanka!" Esther ushered her oldest son, Zechariah, into the family's prayer room. Esther had a total of three children: Zech was the son she prayed for her whole life, while the other two children, Leviticus and Ruth, gave her so many problems. She knew that she'd remained humble, followed God, and was obedient on earth, but she couldn't understand what karma she was getting when she received two children that were always noncompliant to her wishes.

Esther was a single mother and had been that way since her husband left her right after Ruth was born. He claimed it was because he was tired of sharing his wife with another man. That other man happened to be, God. Esther thought that was the most foolish thing she'd ever heard, but she never fought him. She figured if it were meant for them to be together, then he'd return to her. If not, then she had no problem raising her children by herself and that's exactly what she ended up doing.

Esther named each child from a book in the Bible because she considered them all to be Blessings that she never would've had if it weren't for God. She did the best she could to raise them, but sometimes, she felt as though her best wasn't good enough. Being a firm believer in God, she praised herself on being able to raise her children in the church. She believed God was the head of their lives and without Christ nothing would be possible. She tried to instill those same beliefs and values in her children, but they were too defiant to listen or take in anything she said to them.

"Awe man... Momma, why do we have to pray every night?" Zech asked his mother. He often pretended that all the praying that they did bothered him, but that was really a front he put on for his siblings. They complained about everything and when he obeyed, they would pick at him or avoid hanging around him because he went against the grain. You would think that with him being the oldest, nothing that his siblings did bothered him, but it did. Zech wanted them to have a close relationship and if he never sided with them, then he knew that relationship would pretty much remain to be nonexistent.

Zech had no problems with women, but he was quiet and reserved. He liked to stay to himself because he didn't like drama or mess. He'd rather someone not deal with him if they felt they always had to do something that would lead to a fight or could potentially get them put in jail. At eighteen-years-old, Zech was built like a grown man. Six feet, three inches tall with a beautiful set of white teeth, and a milk chocolate skin tone, mixed with an athletic build had women yearning for him, but he overlooked them all. He'd always been focused on his education and walking right in God's eyes. The one thing he always prided himself on was remaining a virgin until he got married. Nobody knew that, and he wanted to keep it that way.

"Because we have to thank God for allowing us to see another day and to ask him to continue to watch over the people we love," his mother responded.

"Okay, but why we gotta do it in the mornings, too? Then, we at church every time they open the doors," Leviticus, the middle child, spoke with haste.

"I'm with you; I get tired of being the only children in church who aren't allowed to have fun. We have to go every Monday and Tuesday for Choir Rehearsal, Wednesday for Bible Study, Thursday for Prayer Meeting,

Friday for Youth Usher Board Rehearsal, Saturday for Children's Day and Member's Meeting, and then go back on Sunday. Even then, we end up going two or three times for both the early morning and regular service and please don't let the Pastor be preaching at an away church…. We have to sit in there and act like we have been saved, sanctified, and filled with the Holy Ghost," their sister, Ruth chimed in. Ruth was the primary problem in the house. Esther felt it was due to her being the baby and only girl. Zech and Levi went overboard with acting as protectors of her. You couldn't even look at her wrong or you'd have to see them.

Ruth was gorgeous in the eyes of her friends and family. Standing at four feet and eleven inches tall, she was what people liked to refer to as "fun-sized"; that was mainly coming from the boys she tended to date. Her complexion was so light that people often mistook her for being mixed and it didn't help that her hair was in the same original curly form that she was born with. Adorned on her face were a full set of pouty lips, dark brown eyes, and deep dimples etched in both of her cheeks. She was stacked in all the right places, which made it easy for her to get a boyfriend and while her family thought she was still a virgin at sixteen, they'd be surprised to learn that she'd been having sex since she was twelve-years-old.

"Ya'll some hardheaded behind children. When you want to go out there and do whatever you want to do, not one of you is complaining. But, every time it's time to give God praise, you seem to have a problem. I didn't raise no heathens, let alone allow none to be baptized. I'm telling each of you now that you better get your life right with God before it's too late," Esther warned them.

"If we pray tonight, can we skip praying all day tomorrow?" Leviticus asked her with a cheesy grin on his face. He meant it as a joke, but Esther didn't see it that way. She was angry at the way he was trying to patronize the things she believed in and tried to teach them.

"I'm not always going to be around. You can make jokes about me wanting each one of you to get closer to the Lord, but y'all better know that He is the truth and the light. Keep on running around here thinking your little behinds don't stank and see what happens. He's going to break every last one of you down, one by one. And when He does..."

"Momma, I'm only sixteen-years-old. There ain't nothing God can say to us that you haven't already told us. Nice try tho," Ruth stood up from the kneeling position she was in to address her mother.

"Where you think you going?" Esther asked.

"Let's be real, Mother. God only blesses those with money. We're so poor, the damn roaches running around here have a better life than us."

"Watch your mouth in my house, Ruth," Esther hollered before she stood as well. She hadn't whipped either of her children in a while, but she wasn't opposed to doing so.

"I'm sorry, Ma. But, let's call a spade a spade. We live in the hood. You're killing yourself working multiple jobs to make sure we have the things we need and some of the things we want. Where was God when he allowed you to get pregnant by a man that would leave you just for loving Him? Where was God when your mother allowed your father to rape you? Yeah, I know all about that. Where was God when you married our father, but he cheated on you religiously? Where was God then?" Esther couldn't understand where all the ill feelings that Ruth was displaying came from, but she was curious to find out.

"Calm down, Child. Just because we don't have the things we want, when we want them, doesn't mean that they we won't get them. We're blessed every day that we get a new chance to open our eyes. Don't you see that?"

"Nope. I don't see anything," Ruth sassed before closing her eyes and pretending to be blind.

"You is one evil heffa," Esther grimaced.

"I'm just being real with you, Ma. I don't see anything, but thanks for trying to put that in the atmosphere," Ruth chided before she walked out the room.

"I'm out too, Ma. Sorry!" Levi spoke before kissing his mother on the cheek. "You coming, Bruh?" he asked Zech.

"Naw, I'ma hang back with Ma. I'll get up with y'all later." He dapped his brother up, then got back in his kneeling position.

"Are you sure you want to be here? I'm not trying to force you into doing anything you don't want to do."

"Ma, I understand what they are saying, and I also get where you're coming from. It may seem like I don't pay attention, but I hear you. I don't see where God has come in and provided us with these blessings that you keep telling us about, but I'm not ready to give up on Him just yet," Zech confessed to his mother. She was happy to hear that. She figured that if she could touch one of her children and teach them about God, then she'd done something right.

"I'm so happy to hear that, Son. Now, do you want to lead prayer, or should I?"

"You can do it."

"Dear God, thank you for allowing us to see another day. You've done things for us that we can't see yet, but we can feel your movement and know that you've made a difference in our lives. You've made sure we had a roof over our head, food on the table, clothes on our back, and plenty of the things that we've asked for, that we never needed. Please guide my children down the right path. I know they don't understand how you've been working in their lives, but the time will come sooner than they think. Thank you so much for allowing us to make it through this day. You've been our shield and protector. I know that you'll never put more on us than we can handle. Watch over our family and friends. Continue to bless us and allow us to live in a way that is acceptable in thine sight. These and all things we ask in thy name. Amen…"

"Amen…" Zech stated behind his mother. "I hate to run, but I need to go check on those other two."

"Be careful, Son," Esther told Zech before watching him exit the room. Esther stayed on her knees a little while longer to say a little extra prayer for her children. They lived in Mobile, Alabama and she knew her children wanted to move to Chicago when they graduated from high school. But, she was scared for them because Chicago wasn't known for being one of the best places to live. Not even staying in the house could keep you safe because as the saying goes, "a bullet doesn't have a name on it." Esther always kept that thought in the back of her mind, which was one of the many reasons she stayed praying for her children and trying to get them to do the right thing.

Esther finished praying and then headed to the kitchen. It was getting late, and she wanted to get dinner started. Knowing her children, they wouldn't be back in the house until at least nine o'clock. It was a school night, so they knew they needed to be in the house and ready for bed by ten o'clock.

Esther paired her cell phone to the radio, so she could listen to her Gospel station on Pandora. She moved through the kitchen singing and dancing without a care in the world. She knew she wasn't the richest, and didn't have everything she wanted, but knew there was someone, somewhere, that had it worse than she did.

"I've been lied on (lied on), cheated (cheated), talked about (talked about), mistreated (mistreated)... I've been used (used), scorned (scorned), talked about sore as a bone...." Esther caught the spirit while listening to her music. *When Long As I Got King Jesus* by Vickie Winans began to play, Esther couldn't control the way her body felt. She started running around the kitchen singing, shouting, and dancing as if she'd caught the Holy Ghost. "Long as I got King Jesus. Long as I got King Jesus. Long... Long... Long... As I got Him, I don't need nobody else..."

Zech and Levi came walking into the kitchen right as their mother began crying like she was about to fall out. They looked on in amusement. Seeing her that way was not a shock or out of character for her, but it seemed to get funnier each time to them. One minute she'd be talking and singing normally; the next minute, she'd be dancing, screaming, and crying. She always told them it was the Holy Spirit taking control of her body, but they always thought it was all in her head.

"Yes, Lord. Thank you, Jesus. Healer. Provider. Protector. Oh, Mighty Jehovah," Esther cried real tears of joy as she began to speak in tongues.

The boys were not use to hearing their mother speaking in tongues; everything else, they were accustomed to. With this being new to them, they looked at her as if she needed to be checked into a mental institution. Esther went on for another ten minutes of crying and praising God for her many blessings. Everything halted when Ruth ran inside the house covered in blood.

"Oh, God! Baby, what's wrong?" Esther ran to Ruth checking to see where she'd been hurt. Zech and Levi followed suit.

"It's not my blood," Ruth quietly stated. That didn't stop everyone from fussing over her and fondling her to see where the blood was coming from. "IT'S NOT MY BLOOD!"

Ruth shouted louder. Everyone stopped touching on her long enough to take in what she'd said.

"If it's not your blood, then whose blood is it?" Zechariah asked.

"It's Libby's blood," Ruth cried. Libby was Ruth's best friend. They'd been rockin' together since their preschool days. To know that something bad happened to her hurt Esther because she knew it'd crush her daughter's heart if she were to lose her best friend.

"What happened?" Esther inquired.

"After I left, I went to go see her. We were sitting on the block smoking we-," Ruth caught herself. "I mean, we were praying and ministering to the people that were passing by," Ruth tried to recover from her previous statement by lying. Normally, Esther would've exploded knowing what her daughter had been up to, but because the situation was so traumatic, she didn't want to upset her daughter any more than she already was.

"Ain't nobody got time for you to be making stuff up and lying. I know when you leave this house that you do what you want because you think you're grown, but you better know that there are consequences to every decision you make. Now, tell me what happened, Chile," Esther fussed.

"We were sitting outside on her mother's car when a guy walked up and started trying to talk to Libby. I kept telling Libby to let him walk away because her boyfriend, Jermaine, was supposed to be on his way to see her and he'd go crazy if he saw another man in her face. Well, Libby didn't listen, as usual." Ruth stopped to collect her thoughts.

"What you stop for? Gon' finish telling us what happened," Esther demanded.

"If you give me a chance to, then I will. You act like this is easy for me," Ruth snapped.

"Ruth Anne Mary Magdalene Jeffries, you better not sass me in a house that I'm paying the bills in, ever again. Now, open your damn mouth and tell me what happened. When nobody don't want you to talk, you'll talk all damn day; now you're acting like a cat got your tongue," Esther ranted.

Ruth knew her mother only cussed when she was upset, so for her to have cussed twice in the same statement, showed her that Esther meant business. She opened her mouth within a matter of seconds to continue telling her family what happened to her best friend.

"Well, like I said... I told her to tell the dude to keep it pushing, but she didn't listen. Naturally, Jermaine's ass popped up and saw them talking. The first thing he did was walk over to them to confront Libby. The guy she was talking to intervened to keep Jermaine from disrespecting her, but that only caused them to get into it more. That's when an altercation happened between all three of them, and Libby was talking cash money noise to Jermaine, telling him that she didn't want to be with him anymore and a whole bunch of other stuff. Jermaine got mad and left. I told Libby that something didn't feel right and that we needed to leave, too, but she wouldn't listen to me. Next thing I knew, Jermaine rode up on us and started shooting. I was able to get out the way, but Libby wasn't so lucky. HE KILLED HER!" Ruth shouted causing tears to fall freely down her face.

Esther wrapped her arms around Ruth and pulled her into her bosom. The tears fell from Ruth's eyes so fast and uncontrollably that the top of Esther's dress was drenched. She didn't care; she was worried about the traumatic stress her daughter was going to experience as a result of seeing her best friend killed.

"Where was He, Ma? Where was He?" Ruth asked out of nowhere, catching her mother off guard.

"Where was who?" Esther probed with confusion.

"Where was this so-called God that's supposed to protect us? Why wasn't He there for Libby?" Esther had no words to explain what Ruth was asking her.

"God makes no mistakes," was the only thing Esther could muster up to say.

"Fuck your GOD! He wasn't there. He's fake. He's as fake as these eyelashes," Ruth yelled before snatching her eyelashes from her eyes. "He's as fake as these Lee press-ons," Ruth continued as she popped off all ten of the fingernails she'd glued on the night before. "He's as fake as these damn extensions in my head. I would pull them out, but they cost too much."

"Girl, you so damn retarded," Levi laughed thinking he could make light of the situation, but neither Esther nor Zech found anything to be funny.

Knock... Knock... Knock...

A knock on the door caused them to panic.

"I wonder who the hell that is," Zech said not thinking about his mother still being in the room with him.

"Excuse me..." Esther squealed with her hands resting on her hips. That was another sign that someone had crossed the line.

Esther was built like the Mrs. Butter-worth 's syrup bottle. She was heavyset, but she still had curves in all the right places. Her skin was the color of dark chocolate, and she wore her hair natural. Women often attacked her, not because of the way she looked, but because she had the type of personality that drew men to her no matter where she went. Whenever you saw her, she'd always be carrying a big, beautiful smile; the type of smile that'd light up a room. However, she was also keen on making different facial expressions to show her emotions, which she had no problem displaying to anyone. That's how her children could pinpoint when her mood would change or when they were walking a fine line with her.

"My bad, Ma. Let me go see who this is," Zech tried to downplay what he'd said before going to the door. "Who is it?" he asked, a little worried that Jermaine had come after Ruth.

"It's Jessica," a soft feminine voice spoke from the opposite side of the door.

"Who?" Zech asked again because he wasn't familiar with the name.

"That's Jessica. You don't know her. I'll get it," Ruth informed them. Zech sighed and backed away from the door to allow Ruth access.

"No, I'll get it," Esther abruptly chimed before she stopped Ruth from standing up. Esther's face expressed worry, but Ruth felt okay letting Jessica in.

"It's okay, Ma. I'm sure she's just coming to check on me. Let me get it," Ruth insisted as she finally stood and continued to the door to open it.

"Hey J-," Ruth started saying as she was opening the front door. Her words were quickly halted as she stared down the barrel of a shiny, gold nine-millimeter.

Pow... Pow...

Two shots went flying towards Ruth. One hit her in the chest; the other hit her in the forehead. Ruth's body instantly dropped to the floor as the person with the gun took off running.

Esther and Zech ran to Ruth, while Levi darted out the door to see if he could catch Jessica. Within five minutes, he jetted back in the house empty-handed. Esther sat on the floor cradling Ruth like she was a newborn baby.

It seemed as though it took forever for the coroner to show up and take Ruth's body away. Her family did not want to let her go, but they had to. Zech and Levi left the house on foot, in search of the person who'd caused the death of their sister.

With the boys gone and Ruth's body already being picked up, Esther made her way to her prayer room. She had all types of emotions running through her. Where was God? How could God not be there when she needed him the most?

"God, how could you? I know I'm not supposed to question your work, I'm supposed to believe that you don't make any mistakes, but this … this one here was a big mistake. You took my daughter away from me. She didn't deserve that. I didn't deserve that. My family didn't deserve that. Why God? Why Ruth? Why my daughter?

How could you turn away from me when I needed you the most? How could you not listen to a mother's prayer?"

Chapter One:

Leviticus

"Aye girl, come holla at me?" Levi called out to Venus. He'd been eyeing her since he stepped foot on the campus of the University of Chicago, but she always played him to the left. The fact that he had a girlfriend didn't help him out either.

"My name ain't girl," she replied, rolling her eyes.

"Then what's yo name?"

"Nunya?"

"Nunya? What the hell kind of name is that?"

"It's exactly the way it sounds. Nunya... As in, nun ya damn business," she smirked and walked away.

"I swear these bitches ain't worth a damn these days," he stated to himself.

"What bitches?" Out of nowhere, Levi's girlfriend, Ariana, popped up wanting to know what he was fussing about.

"Nobody, Baby. This girl was tripping about helping me with our pop quiz earlier," he lied to cover himself.

"Uh huh. If you'd been studying instead of hanging out with Tez and Taz, then you would be able to pass your quiz without needing any help."

Tez and Taz were twins that Levi and Zech met when they first arrived on campus. They used to be stuck together like glue, but when Levi picked up another group of friends, he stopped hanging around the twins so much. Not only that, but the twins didn't approve of Levi's choice of extra-curricular activities. Levi decided to avoid them, so he wouldn't have to worry about them judging him. He received enough judgement from people he didn't know; he didn't need it from his friends, too.

"Ain't nobody been hanging out with nobody. You trippin'" he said.

"Yeah... Yeah... Whatever you say," she responded before walking away.

"Where you think you going?" he asked, jogging up beside her.

"I'm going to go see my man."

"Your man? That nigga ain't me."

"I know he ain't because my man is a genius. He wouldn't need someone to help him with his quiz," she laughed.

"I swear I can't stand you," Levi cracked as he wrapped his arms around her. At times, they liked to play with each other through different role-playing activities. That was one of the ways they kept excitement in their relationship. Levi admired Ariana's body as they walked. It caused him to think back to when they first met.

On his first day, the campus was open for incoming freshmen; he was walking around the campus trying to familiarize himself with where everything was. Especially, his classes so he wouldn't be stuck trying to look for them on the first day of school. As he walked through campus, he spotted Ariana sashaying into the student union. Inside that building were a couple of restaurants, offices, and the bookstore. As he watched her approach the door, he took off running trying to catch up to her, fearing if he didn't speak to her then, he'd never see her again.

"Sup Lil momma?"

"I'm not your momma and I'm not a lil girl, so don't step to me like that."

"Chill boo. I didn't mean any harm. I'm just trynna get to know you."

"How do you know I don't have a man or that I'm not lesbian?" she sassed.

"If you had a man, we wouldn't have gotten this far in our conversation, and if you were into women, you would've cut me off and told me that from the jump." Ariana didn't respond. She took some time to get her mind right before saying anything.

"You don't know me, so don't stand there trying to analyze me," she fussed.

"You ain't gotta come at me like that. If you ain't got the time or don't want to talk to me, then that's all you had to say. I'm a whole grown ass man; I don't play childish games," he retorted before he turned to walk away. He didn't take two steps before he was yanked back towards Ariana.

"Calm yo ass down," Ariana stated, catching him off guard. "This conversation ain't over until I say it's over. Now, what's your name?" Her asking him that was the start of a beautiful relationship. Of course, Ariana made him take things slow and made sure he was serious about

her. She let him know up front that she wasn't with the shits and had no problem dropping him quick if she had to. Levi didn't need an example; he'd seen everything he needed to see when they first interacted, for him to be able to analyze her. She was bipolar and surely certifiable, so he wasn't about to take no chances of playing with her and end up swimming with the fishes.

"Hey, Baby! How was your day?" he finally asked, after they were able to stop laughing and he'd been able to return from his thoughts of the past.

"Long. I'm glad that it's over. How was yours?"

"It was cool. I missed you," he informed her while kissing her forehead.

"I can tell. You ain't let me go since you pulled me into this hug," she cracked.

"Fine. See if I try loving on you again," he joked while pushing her off him.

"Whatever. What do you want to get to eat?"

"I really wanna stay in and have a Firestick and chill night with you."

"Firestick and chill? Really tho?"

"Yes, Baby. You know that Netflix is played out," he honestly stated. "Let's go back to your house. I'd say we could go to my dorm, but you already know my roommate won't leave."

"I swear he needs to get a life. He just hasn't been the same for how long now?"

"Mannnn... Ever since Ruth died, he became a completely different person." By him, he was referring to his brother, Zechariah. Since the day they witnessed Ruth take her last breath, he had secretly been on a revenge kick. Zechariah thought no one knew what he was up to, but Levi knew Zech was willing to go to the end of the earth to find out who killed their sister so that he could watch them take their last breath.

"Yeah, I know. He'll come around," Ariana stated, doing her best to make Levi feel a little better about the tragic event that changed the dynamics of their entire family.

"I hope so. I already lost my sister. Never thought I'd lose my brother, too. Let me not even get started on my mother. She was big in the church then, but she's overdoing it now. It's crazy."

It had been four years since Ruth's murder inside their home. As far as they knew, someone named Jessica knocked on the door to kill their sister, but they'd never met her before, so they didn't have any information to give the police. Well, other than the only name they could think of, Jessica.

He tightened his grip on Ariana and tried his best to push back the tears that were threatening to fall from his eyes. He was still dealing with Ruth's death the best way he knew how. He didn't feel like anything he was doing was helping. He considered seeing a psychiatrist, but he felt they wouldn't do anything, but judge him. He'd been judged too many times in life to allow another person to do it, too.

"Okay, Baby. Let me run to the store to get something to cook, then you can come over. Give me about an hour," Ariana told him.

"Cool, I'ma go check on my brother, I'll see you shortly," he returned, before kissing Ariana one last time, and bidding her farewell.

Walking back to his dorm, Leviticus thought about his life and how he graduated high school and opted to go off to college because he felt it was the only way he'd be able to make something out of himself and get away from the hood. He received a full academic scholarship to the University of Chicago, where he was double majoring in Business Administration and Social Work. His intended goal was to create a business that would allow him to help troubled youth. Starting a program to encourage them not to join gangs, and see that they had a bright future ahead of them.

By the time his mind was cleared from his thoughts, he'd made it to his dorm. He decided to take the steps up to his room instead of the elevator because he knew he was on limited time. When he reached the 3rd floor, he sprinted towards his room. He was glad his brother had left the door unlocked cause didn't have to dig through his book bag to locate his key, which he was sure that he'd left in the room earlier that morning.

"What's up, Bro?"

"Ain't nothin'. Where you been?" Zech asked.

"In class where you should've been. What you are gonna tell momma when she calls and asks about your grades?"

"The same thing I always tell her; that I'm good and I got this. Worry about yourself, fool," Zech joked.

"Uh huh, but you better know that when she asks me about you, I'm telling."

"Ole snitch ass. That's cool tho. Now, come on so we can get this money," Zech instructed.

Levi wasted no time throwing his book bag on his bed and heading out the door behind his brother. He knew what they were about to do was wrong, but they needed the money, so he made up in his mind that as usual, he'd do what he wanted to, act as if his behaviors weren't too severe, and then pray to ask God to forgive him later.

Chapter Two:

Zechariah

On their way to meet up with their homeboy, Zech found himself drowning his brother out. He didn't understand why Levi always saw the need to butt into his business or call himself worrying about him when he kept telling him that he could take care of himself.

"When do you think we should go home and check on momma?"

"Break."

"What break?"

"Christmas."

"Why are you so short with me?"

"Because I'm tired of you asking so many questions. Worry about yourself. I got me," he voiced, quickly shutting Levi down. He wasn't doing it to be mean, but he was tired of feeling like people were babying him.

Before they knew it, they were pulling up in front of Amp's house. Amp was who they liked to consider their connect. He would tell them about opportunities out there where they could all make money.

"What up, lil' niggas?" Amp walked outside inquiring. Not one time did he leave his porch.

Zech and Levi stepped out the car and made their way towards Amp's porch. Before they could make it all the way up the steps, a car pulled up in the driveway. Both of the boys turned around to see who it was. Zech was in awe when he made eye contact with one of the women that stepped out. There were only two women present, but the one on the passenger side was the one who caught his eye. She appeared before him standing at five feet, seven inches tall with calves the size of soft balls indicating to him that she either worked out or did a lot of muscle toning exercises. As he studied her body from her head to her feet, he adored every curve that graced her. She had to be a size sixteen and what he'd like to refer to as slim-thick. The tight curls on her head added to her beauty and added volume to her somewhat chubby face, but it was angelic and one of the most beautiful faces he'd ever seen."

"You coming in or you going to stand here looking crazy, Mia?"

"You go ahead, Jaclyn. You know I don't feel comfortable walking in Amp's house. He's too crazy for me and has too much unnecessary drama going on every time we turn around," Mia responded.

"Girl, you too much for me. I don't know why you always want to tag along with me when you already know where I am going and then you get in the car and complain the whole ride. That's ridiculous and annoying as hell. Anyway, I'll be right back, let me just run this to Amp," Jaclyn informed her before grabbing a book bag from the backseat of her car and heading towards where Amp was standing.

"You going to say something to her or you plan on staring a hole through her?" Levi whispered to Zech.

"Man, if you don't watch back. I got me; worry about you."

"Hey guys," Jaclyn seductively spoke when she walked passed the boys. She walked up on Amp and attempted to place a kiss on his lips.

"Aye, chill out with that. You know I'm not about to play with you; I don't know where your lips have been so don't come trying to kiss all on me," Amp fussed. Jaclyn put her head down. She'd tried on more than one occasion to try to be the leading lady in Amp's life, but he turned her down more times than she could count.

Jaclyn wasn't a bad looking woman. She stood at five feet and nine inches tall. Most men were often intimidated because of her height, but she had no problem letting anyone know how much she loved being tall. Being the color of brown sugar, she always rocked twenty-two, twenty-four, and twenty-six inched Brazilian bundles in her hair. People often wondered how she could afford such good hair, but she'd never tell a soul about any of her side hustles. Mia was her best friend, and even she didn't know. Another problem that men often had with Jaclyn was that she had a few cracked teeth and halitosis. She walked around thinking she was better than everyone else and her attitude was not the best.

"Oh, so now you don't hear me talking to you? That's exactly why I don't like dealing with you," Amp roared, trying to get Jaclyn to see how much she was pissing him off.

"I hear your hypocritical ass, but I don't feel the need to respond to it," she admitted.

"And why is that? Because you don't like to hear the truth about the way people view you. It ain't no secret that you a whole hoe and for that very reason, I don't want those suckers anywhere near my face," he asserted, pointed towards her lips.

"That's quite funny that you don't want me kissing on you, but you'll put me on my back any chance you can get."

"I'm a man, what do you expect? I'll never turn down cat, whether it's good or bad. Furthermore, you don't have to kiss someone to have sex with them. If you believe that you do, then I feel sorry for you," he acknowledged to her.

"Whatever. Let's get this over with so I can get on to somebody that has time for me."

"Yeah, you do that."

They stood on the porch for what seemed like forever, eyeballing each other before they finally walked inside the house to finish out their little transaction. They didn't want anybody to see what they were up to or hear what needed to be discussed between them.

While that was taking place, Zech continued to admire Mia. Levi grew tired of watching his brother shamefully stare at Mia, so he took it upon himself to talk to her. He figured if Zech saw him over there, he'd get jealous and step his game up.

"Aye bro, where you going?"

"To get you a woman." Levi smiled at his brother and kept marching towards Mia who was leaned up against Jaclyn's car.

"Oh Lord," Mia stated out loud, even though she thought she was talking to herself.

"Don't be like that, Ma. I'm just trying to get to know you, so I can see if you're good enough for my brother."

"Good enough for your brother? Boy, please! I know you not talking about the dude over there that's been staring at me like he's slow or something."

"Baby, I'm far from slow," Zech finally walked towards her and joined in on the conversation.

"I can't tell. All you've done was stare at me since I've gotten out the car. Do I know you or something?"

"I dunno, do you?" Zech called himself being smart, but all he did was get on her nerves.

"Look, what do you want? I've never been the one to play games with other folk's children, and I'm not about to start now."

"You ain't gotta play with me, but I can assure you that I have no problems playing with you and that's in and out of the bedroom," Zech assured her.

Levi stood back shaking his head at the way his brother came off while talking to Mia. Even he could see that she wasn't the type of woman that would play games with him or fall for the cheap pick-up lines.

"You know what... I'm not even about to go there with you. You think I'm desperate for some attention or something? You think because I'm big that I can't get a man to come to me with some respect?" Mia started popping off at the mouth because she was offended by the way that Zech had spoken to her. He didn't mean any harm, but he didn't know what else to say to her. He'd used a line that he heard some man say on a comedic sketch on YouTube.

"He didn't mean anything by it, Ma. He's new to this macking stuff, so cut him a little slack," Levi stepped in trying to help his brother out.

"Is that right?"

"That's what I said, ain't it?"

"Well, since you said that..." Mia sashayed closer to Zech and put her chest close to his. He almost fell backwards feeling her get close up on him.

"Wha-wha-what are you doing?" He was so nervous that the only thing he could do was stutter.

"Don't get scared, Baby. You said you could handle me in and out the bedroom, so I wanna know how you plan on doing that." Mia continued to taunt Zech, but all it did was make his manhood begin to rise in his pants. He didn't know what to do. Mia looked down and started shaking her head before she retreated to the car. By that time, Jaclyn was headed back out the house.

"Damn bruh, I can't believe you messed that up like that."

"Don't start with me. She probably wasn't worth my time anyway," Zech mumbled, trying to make light of the situation, even though he was upset at the way he'd been rejected. Zech hated being rejected and it normally didn't turn out well for the person that did the rejecting. He was big on revenge since his sister died. It didn't matter what you did to him, if it was something he didn't approve of or think was funny, then he'd find a way to get retribution from the person that embarrassed him.

"My bad, Bruh. You really need some of that fat monkey she looks like she got, too." Zech couldn't help but laugh at his brother because he knew he was right; Mia did look like she was walking around with a fat cat and at some point, he'd love the chance to experience feeling it.

Before Ruth's death, Zech was a virgin. He'd planned on staying that way until he settled down with someone and was ready to have and able to care of children. However, when he started stepping away from his faith, he started passing his rod around like he was passing a collection plate. He didn't care who he was with, when he was with them, or even if he used protection. It had gotten so bad, that he prayed upon getting AIDS so that he could die and join his sister. However, as time went by, he saw the error of his ways and began to be more careful with whom he gave his body to.

"I can admit that I'm a little dusty with trying to talk to women, but I'm not going to chase her or kiss her ass. Either she wants to talk to me, or she doesn't. And I can assure you that no matter what decision she makes, I'll still be good."

"I hear you, and I don't doubt that you won't be good. However, I've seen you alone for far too long. It's time you find somebody that's going to love and cherish you. I think that's the one thing you've been missing since Ruth died."

"Don't bring her into this. This has nothing to do with her," Zech raised his voice.

"Keep telling yourself that lie. This has everything to do with us losing our sister. If that never would've happened, you wouldn't have shut down on everyone the way you have, and we would've all been in a better place with our lives," Levi explained.

"As I said before, I appreciate you looking out for me, but I'm good."

"Fine, but at least do this. Let me pull Jaclyn to the side so you'll get a few minutes alone with Mia. I know you say you're not going to chase her or kiss her ass, which I've not one time asked you to do; I'd never ask you to do either of those things. But, I do think you should try to talk to her again before they leave; I promise I'll keep Jaclyn busy for a couple of minutes, so gon' over there and handle your business."

Zech spent a few brief minutes deliberating on the things that his brother said to him. He was truly tired of being stuck in his room a lot because he didn't want to be around people he didn't know or care for, but at the same time, he wanted companionship. He'd love to explore things with Mia to see where they could go, but he knew that he was going to have to take things super slow and he was fine with that. He just hoped that if she were onboard with giving him a chance, then she would be willing to take her time too.

"Aight. Good lookin' out," Zech told Levi before dapping him up. He knew at times that it appeared that he didn't like his brother, but he truly did love and appreciate him for always having his back. "And by the way, thanks bruh. I appreciate you from the bottom of my heart." A smile spread across Levi's face as he received his brother's gratitude. He wasn't the sappy type, so he knew hugging his brother was out of the question.

"You don't have to thank me; that's what brothers are for," Levi confirmed before going to stop Jaclyn before she reached Mia. "Come here and let me holla at cha, Jaclyn," Levi gestured.

"What you want with me?"

"Come here, hell." He was annoyed with her. Zech just stood back to see what his brother was about to do.

"What you want?"

"Give me yo girl's number."

"I know you didn't come at me to ask for another chick's number," Jaclyn sassed. She showed that she was pissed that the only reason he had stepped to her was that he was interested in Mia.

"It's for my brother. He likes her, and I'm tired of him being alone."

"What do I get out the deal?"

"What you want?" he asked, pulling out a stack of cash to count her off a bill or two.

"Naw, I don't want your money. I want some of this," she returned before grabbing a handful of his manhood.

He jumped back stunned at how forward she was. Now, he knew exactly why Amp didn't want to get down with her. If she'd throw it to him that easily, ain't no telling who else she'd be willing to throw her cat to.

"It ain't that type of party, Ma. I got a girl," he informed her, although they both knew that even with him having a woman, he was never the type to stick to just one woman.

"You think that's supposed to faze me? Guess again. Now, if I don't get what I want, you won't get what you want," she had no problem propositioning him. She used one of her fingers to run a trail from his lips, down to his groin.

"I'm good, Ma. Gon' with yo friend," he instructed before heading back towards his brother who was still standing there. Zech was laughing so hard at him that tears began to flow down his face.

"What's so funny? I was trying to help you out." Zech was laughing so hard that he couldn't get any words out. "Yeah, keep laughing. I'ma be laughing tonight, too, when

I'm deep inside Ariana, and you're sitting there with your lotion in one hand and Johnson in the other."

"Noooo... Don't get mad at me because she tried you the way you've done women for years. You mean to tell me that the player of all players has an issue with someone trying to pick him up?"

"Whatever. I'm not desperate you knew I wasn't trying to holla at that hood rat. I was only trying to do you a favor, but I won't do it again." Levi turned and headed towards the porch as Amp returned.

After witnessing Jaclyn and Mia drive away, Zech stood there remembering Mia's beauty before he told himself, "She may think she got away from a nigga, but she'll soon learn that I always get what I want." After giving himself that minor pep talk, he headed back to the porch to join Levi and Amp, so they could continue to get their plans together for the hit they were planning that night.

Chapter Three:

Mia

"Let's go, Jaclyn," Mia told her friend as soon as she got to the car.

"Get in so we can go then," Jaclyn responded while rolling her eyes.

Mia didn't comment on the attitude Jaclyn had given her. She knew it was only due to the fact that Levi had asked Jaclyn about her. But, she felt that was stupid for Jaclyn to get mad when she didn't even know the whole story.

With both women in the car, they rode in silence on their way back to the campus. Mia's stomach began to growl, so she knew she needed to get something to eat. It didn't help that she was diabetic, and it was already pass the time for her to eat and take her nightly dose of medication.

"Are you really mad at me?"

"Mad at you for what?"

"For talking to Levi and Zech? You know that Levi doesn't want me."

"Could've fooled me. What he ask for your number for?"

A Mother's Prayer

"Because his brother Zech was trying to talk to me, but it didn't work out if his favor. Levi asking you for my number was for his brother, which is what he told you."

"And I'm supposed to believe that?"

"You can believe what you want to believe, but we've been friends for years. When can you ever tell me a time that I crossed you or betrayed your trust as a friend?" Mia waited on Jaclyn to respond. After ten minutes of still being in silence, Mia decided to speak again. "You can't say anything because you know I'd never do anything that would mess up our friendship. Now, if you want to continue to be a bi-." Jaclyn shot Mia a cold stare, which caused Mia to not even finish getting the word out.

"All I'm saying is that Levi doesn't want me. He told you that and so did I. If you were so concerned that we were lying about that, then why didn't you just ask Zech about it when he was standing in your presence?"

"It don't even matter. I don't want to talk about it anymore."

"Fine. Then let's talk about what it was you had to do with Amp when you walked inside his house."

"Why you always. Being nosey. What I do and who I do it with, ain't got nothing to do with you."

"Jaclyn, you my girl and everything, but you not about to continue to talk to me crazy. Now, I told you that Levi don't want me, and I don't want him. His brother is interested in me and I actually think he's kind of cute, too. Now, either you can help me get with him or not. Either way, I got me."

"Well, I'm glad to know you got you because I'm not getting involved with that. Now, what you want to eat? I know you hungry because your stomach is growling like a bear," Jaclyn finally laughed.

"You know I despise your ass, right? I can't stand the way you try to be mean one minute and an angel the next minute."

"Girl bye! You know you love me like everyone else does. Now, what do you want to eat?"

"I actually have a taste for a good Philly cheese steak."

"Me, too. Let's go to Monti's."

"Are you sure you want to go that far?"

"It's really not that far to me. Plus, I don't want to go back to campus right now," Jaclyn rasped.

"Fine. Let's go then. But, tell me what you can about Zech and Levi."

"I know they country as hell. They are actually from Alabama."

"Oh, really. I have some relatives that live down that way. What part are they from?"

"Oh, I'm not sure. I don't really talk to them like that and that's all I really know about them. I've been trying to talk to Levi for a while now because I've heard a few things about him from some women on the campus, but every time he gets around me, he wants to pull out that girlfriend card," Jaclyn snarled as she turned her nose up in disgust.

Mia laughed at Jaclyn because she knew she hated the fact that she couldn't pull Levi. Especially, with Jaclyn had always been the type of female that could pretty much pull any man that she tried to sink her paws into. The fact that Levi didn't want her said a lot and was actually a good thing for him. Jaclyn was far from a saint and had done more men than probably a prostitute, but Mia never judged her.

"Mia, do you remember that speech you said when we were in that creative writing class?" Jaclyn probed.

"What speech?"

"The one where you were talking about how strange things were. It made a lot of sense to me and it's really plagued my mind over the past few days."

"And why is that?"

"I dunno. It just seems like I need to get my life together. But, can you say it for me again?"

"Sure. But, I don't think me telling you that will help you get closer to God," Mia acknowledged.

"Who said anything about getting closer to God? I said I needed to get my life together. Plus, I already feel like I'm close to God. Just because I don't pray in front of people, don't mean that I don't pray."

"And you think that prayer is the only way to get close to God?"

"It is in my book. Now, stop trying to patronize me and just do what I said. I need to hear it."

"Okay, but as long as you know that hearing it won't change your life, then we good."

"I know that it won't and I'm fine with that. But, sometimes we just need to hear things to help us gain a better understanding of certain things and to help us feel better."

"Oh okay... Well I can do that."

"Good, I'm listening," Jaclyn stated. Mia looked at her for a while wondering what could've been going on with her before she opened her mouth and began to talk.

"It's Strange...."

"Wait... It's that the name of it?"

"Yes, that's the name of it. Now, can you stop interrupting me, so I can get it out," Mia fussed.

"Don't be such an ass about it. Sheesh... Go ahead," Jaclyn snapped back. Mia rolled her eyes before continuing.

"It's Strange... It's strange how twenty dollars seems like such a large amount when you donate it to church, but such a small amount when you go shopping. It's strange how two hours seem so long when you're at church, and how short they seem when you're watching a good movie. It's strange that you can't find words to say when you're praying, but you have no trouble thinking what to talk about with a friend. It's strange how difficult it is to read one chapter of the Bible, but how easy it is to read a popular novel. It's strange how we need to know about an event for church two to three weeks before the day, so we can include it in our agenda, but we can adjust it for other events in the last minute? It's strange how difficult it is to learn a fact about God and share it with others, but it's easy to repeat gossip. It's strange how we believe everything that magazines and newspapers say, but we question the words in the Bible?" Mia's eyes remained closed the entire time she recited the short saying because she didn't want to say anything wrong and her eyes being closed helped her to concentrate.

"Did you write that?"

"No, I found it in a magazine once and I memorized it from there. I can't remember who came up with it, but they were truthful through its entirety."

"I agree with you. It makes a lot of since and those things are strange. I'm one of those people who think things are bad when it comes down to going to church, but I'll do anything I want to do and not have a complaint in the world," Jaclyn confessed.

"We all have moments like that and the minute we realize it and are prepared to build that relationship with God, the sooner we begin to see greater changes in our lives," Mia preached.

The girls rode the remainder of the way to Monti's talking about God and the church. Jaclyn felt a storm coming and disclosed those feelings to Mia. Mia let her know that she'd always have her back, even in her time of need and that if she ever needed to talk, she was there for her. She even had Jaclyn pull over on the side of the road so that she could say a quick prayer for her.

Mia was focused on making sure her friend was good, but she was also still thinking about Zech. She knew she'd played hard to get with him, but she silently prayed that she didn't play too hard.

Chapter Four:

Leviticus

Levi quickly became agitated at his phones constant buzzing. He knew that it was only Ariana because he was supposed to have been at her house over an hour ago, but he had bigger fish to fry. When Amp called, they answered because he was the main source of their income. He thought back to the day he was first hooked up with him.

Leviticus went to a job interview with Xfinity. He wanted to get a job as a customer service representative so that when he and his brother got their own place, he'd be able to get free cable. However, while he was at the interview and they told him what the pay was, he decided it wasn't the job for him. There was no way he could work a job where customers could be rude, and disrespectful to him for a measly nine dollars an hour. After the interview, he was walking to his car and he noticed this bad ass 2013 Dodge Challenger sittin' on twenty-twos with dark tinted windows. Amp was sitting inside watching porn, which you could see once you'd gotten up on it.

"Damn bro, she really handling that meat. Where you find that one?" Levi started Amp.

"Aye, don't be walking up on me like that. You don't know if I was packing or not."

"My bad. I just wanted to know where you got that movie from. I ain't seen that one before and I love Pinky's big thick ass."

"Yeah, she is bad, huh? But, I got the hookup. I get any and every movie I want for little of nothing. What you know about porn youngster?"

"It's been my favorite movie genre since I was about eleven," Levi chuckled, causing Amp to laugh with him.

"I hear ya. Where you from?"

"Alabama... Mobile to be exact. That's down there close to the Mississippi Gulf Coast."

"Oh okay. I got some folks down that way, but I don't get down with them like that."

"In Alabama?"

"Naw, on the coast. But like I said, I don't get down with them like that," Amp reiterated.

"Oh, word? Well, I'm sure whatever the reason was, it was a damn good one."

"What makes you think that?" Amp challenged, waiting for Levi to try to slip up and say the wrong thing.

"Because I'm big on family and loyalty and you seem like the type of person that's big on it, too. So if you don't get down with yours, then there's a reason for that." Levi chimed, trying to play it cool. Even though they'd just met, Levi swore he was good at reading people.

"Yeah, loyalty means a lot to me, so I have no problem handling people when they try to screw me over," Amp warned.

"You don't have to worry about that, homie. Unless you rocking a slit between your legs and no I'm not talking about the one in your shaft, then we ain't got nothing to discuss in those regards."

"In what regards?"

"In the regards of me trying to screw you," Levi chuckled.

"Aight. That sounds good to me." Levi may have played things cool, but on the inside, he knew that he needed to watch Amp. Initially, he had good vibes about Amp.

However, the more they talked, the more something didn't sit too well with him.

They chopped it up for a few more minutes and exchanged contact information. Amp told Levi that he could put him up on how to get some money. Levi was worried that Amp was going to get him involved in some shit that would get him a life sentence. But with him being unable to find a job and his mother not being able to send him and his brother enough money to make it at school, he knew he had to do something. Ever since that day, he'd been kicking it with Amp hard. The only reason he thought to include his brother in what he was doing was that he wanted to get him out the dorms. It wasn't the best thing for either of them, but he knew he needed to get Zech out of that room before he went crazy and he ended up losing the brother he'd known his entire life.

"Y'all ready or nah?" Zech interrupted them. He was more than ready to do what they had to do so that he could get back to the dorms. Hearing his brother speak, brought Levi back from his random memory.

"Yeah, my bad. Let's get out of here."

"Naw, I'm not going this time. You've gotta handle this one yourselves," Amp told them.

"What you mean? You always go with us! This better not be no setup," Levi hollered out in anger. He couldn't even say why he was mad, but something felt off about the situation.

Ever since the first time he went out with Amp, he was scared that he'd get caught up in some mess. He wanted the money, but he wanted his freedom more. With Amp always being by his side, it made things appear to be a lot easier to do. Now, with Amp saying he wasn't going, things seemed a bit fishy to Levi. For Amp to not go, that meant that everything would go to him and Zech and he knew that Amp wasn't the kind of man to pass up any money.

"What reason do I have to set you up? I got something else that I need to check into that could potentially be an even bigger hit next week. You need to chill out and take some of that bass out of your voice when you're talking to me. I don't know who you think you're talking to," Amp quickly jumped into defense mode to defend himself.

"Whatever man, give us the address so we can get this over with. How long do we have?"

"They shouldn't be back until around 10:00 tonight. It's a little after seven, and it should take you about twenty minutes to get there. Once you get the alarm clipped, you need to park in the garage and grab all the big shit," Amp instructed. The brothers nodded at him before heading to his garage to get inside the big fifteen passenger van that they used to carry all of their stolen goods.

"You switched the tags out?" Zech asked right as he slid in the passenger seat.

"Naw. I forgot. Hang tight," Levi responded as he hopped out the driver side to change out the license plates.

Amp was considered to be their hook-up to all of the places they would hit up. He worked for an alarm company and was able to pretty much get into anybody's house that dealt with their company. Of course, to qualify for their alarm systems, the customer had to have good credit, and most of the times, Amp pinpointed them to be senior citizens or the wealthy. That was right up their alley because it allowed them to break into these people's homes and take things worth monetary value and be able to make it through at least a good four months before they'd have to go out and steal again. They knew it was wrong, but they needed the money and would do anything they had to do to get it.

Amp purchased an old van from a man off Facebook marketplace and fixed it up a few years back. They'd often go through the parking garage at downtown businesses to take license plates off cars, so they'd have some to switch on the van so that when the police were looking for it, they wouldn't be quick to point them out. They would even go as far as painting the van after every two jobs to decrease the chances of them getting caught. It'd worked in their favor for the past two years, so they figured it was no sense in switching up the routine.

Once Levi had the plates switched, he hopped back in the van and programmed the address into his GPS on his phone. It took exactly twenty minutes before they got to the home. It was dark outside, but the neighborhood had lights everywhere. They noticed a neighborhood watch sign that they hadn't seen the few times they'd been in that neighborhood prior.

"You sure we at the right place?"

"Yeah man. I put it in Google Maps the way he gave it to me. Why? You getting scared?"

"Man, it ain't never been this jumpin' over here," Zech acknowledged.

"I know. I wonder what the hell is up."

The boys drove around the neighborhood once to get a feel of what could be up before finally parking in front of the house they were originally supposed to be at. They noticed that almost every light in the house was on, which was strange. Normally, people in that neighborhood only had lights on when they were home.

"Why you park directly in front of the house? You know you gonna give us away!"

"How am I gonna give us away? If someone comes, we can always say we have the wrong house."

"Naw, I think you need to move the van. You making us too noticeable."

"Would you stop being a crybaby7. Hold on and let me go knock to see if anyone's home," Levi suggested. He opened the door to get out, but his brother grabbed his hand. "What you grabbing me for, fool?"

"Chill out and wait. Something ain't right."

They sat in the car for three minutes before Zech yelled out, "Push the gas."

That was all he had to say. Levi threw the car in drive and punched the gas getting the hell out of the neighborhood.

"What happened?"

"That just ain't feel right. Something wasn't right about this entire situation. We need to ditch this van," Zech advised.

Doing as his brother suggested, Levi maneuvered through town as discreetly as possible, before heading to a park. They jumped out the van, being sure to take off their shirts and wipe it down. They even took the tag off the back of it to prevent leaving any fingerprints behind.

"This way, man," Zech barked out orders, guiding them from where they were, back to a neighborhood close to the school.

"How the hell did you know to come this way?"

"You think I sit in that dorm all day, but I can assure you that I do way more than that. Now, how the hell are we supposed to get Amp back for this?"

"Back for what? We don't even know if anything was about to go down."

"You've got to be crazy as hell if you don't see we were just set-up. I'm pretty sure 5-0 was on him, so he sent them our way," Zech asserted, but his brother wasn't trying to hear anything he had to say.

"Amp ain't showed me nothing but loyalty. Until I see different, then ain't no way I'm going to think he did something as foul as what you're claiming he did."

"Fine, don't believe me. But, when they have you thrown under the jail, don't be sitting there looking stupid."

When they made it back to the campus, the boys parted ways. Leviticus headed to see Ariana while Zechariah headed back to the dorm. Levi had to take public transportation to get to Ariana's house because he'd left his car parked at Amp's crib and he didn't want to bother his brother anymore that night. Levi knew it was going to be an issue once he and Ariana we face to face. She'd been waiting for him, calling him, and he'd been ignoring all her calls.

By the time he arrived at Ariana's house, she was sitting on her porch with an evident attitude. When she saw him walking up the driveway, she stood and started pacing back and forth.

"Where the hell have you been?"

"Here we go," Levi mumbled to himself before he threw on a smile and prepared to butter her up as he did every other time she'd gotten mad at him.

Chapter Five:

Ariana

"Hey baby," Levi walked up on her trying to wrap his arms around her.

"Get away from me. You're not about to get away with this like I let you do everything else."

"Come on, Baby. Let me explain."

"Let you explain? LET YOU EXPLAIN? How the hell do you plan on explaining to me how you constantly disrespect our relationship? What nigga were you with this time?"

"Come on, Ariana. Calm down, Baby."

"Don't tell me to calm down. You know what, I'm not about to do this with you. You keep running around here with these so-called friends of yours who don't mean you any good. You keep standing me up when our relationship has been hanging on by a string for a while. If you can't see that, then obviously this relationship hasn't been that important to you for quite some time now," she ranted.

Pacing back and forth, she continued to go on and on about every issue she's been having with him and their relationship for the past few months. He stood there and listened to her for as long as he cared to before he grabbed her up and pushed her inside of her house. It wasn't that he was trying to hurt her, but he wanted to get her inside before any more of her nosey neighbors stepped outside and got in their business.

"What are you doing? Get your hands off me."

"Shut up, Ariana. I've heard enough of your mouth, and now you're about to hear mine. You think I don't know what's wrong with you?"

"What are you talking about?" she asked, putting her head down causing her chin to touch her chest. She was hoping and praying that he didn't know the one secret she'd been keeping from him.

"You can't bullshit me. I know when something isn't right with you and we've been together long enough for me to know your body and the way it functions. So, try again with playing somebody stupid," he barked.

Ariana didn't open her mouth. Instead, she stood before her man and admired his body that she loved so much. He was the man she'd always dreamed of being with despite knowing her parents would look at him and immediately be against her relationship. Even though her family was African American, they felt that the average African American male would never be good enough for her and that she needed to find someone outside of her race. Ariana didn't agree with them, and for that reason, she moved away from her family to go to school and live the life she wanted.

While Levi continued to talk, she stared his six-foot, one-inch frame up and down. He was the color of milk chocolate with an athletic build. His haircut low, tapered on the sides and waves that reminded her of the sea. He rocked a full beard that he kept lined to perfection. What captivated her the most was that beautiful smile and that pearly white grill. This man was everything to her. Not to mention, he had the same deep dimples etched in both of his cheeks as his sister, Ruth, once had.

"Are you listening to me?" Levi probed. His question brought her back from her thoughts of him.

"Huh? Oh, yeah; I'm listening," she lied. There was no way she could tell him she didn't care about anything he was saying. She didn't feel like hearing him scold her like she was his two-year-old daughter.

"When were you going to tell me about the baby?"

"Baby? What baby?"

"Cut the crap, Ariana. I know that you're pregnant and I've known for a while. Were you not going to tell me about it?" he roared. She could tell that he was upset, but she somewhat didn't care. It was her body, and as far as she was concerned, she could do whatever she wanted with it.

Ariana learned a few months ago that she was pregnant. She hadn't told anyone about it because she didn't want to be judged for having a child without being married. She'd been keeping this secret for months, she hadn't even told the people closest to her, her sister, or her best friend, and they shared everything. She wanted to wait until the right time, which was after she decided what she was going to do before she told anyone; including Levi.

"Answer the damn question... WHEN WERE YOU GOING TO TELL ME THAT YOU WERE PREGNANT?"

"I wasn't.... I wasn't going to tell you anything until I knew what was going to happen?"

"What you mean until you knew what was going to happen?"

"Look at us, Levi. We can't get us right for anything. All we've been doing is fighting lately."

"No, you need to correct that. All you've been doing lately is yelling, and I've been listening. I don't argue because I don't do the back and forth, so you can try using that excuse with someone else."

"You know that things haven't been right with us."

"That's because you've been trying to be my mother and not my woman. I have a mother, I don't need or want another one. Now, sit the hell down so we can talk because you are talking real foul right now and I don't like it," he barked.

"You don't get to tell me what to do, now or ever. Do you understand that? I'm not about to play these games with you. You don't control me. I won't allow you to treat me like you did those other broads you dealt with."

"SIT YOUR ASS DOWN, NOW!!!"

"I'm not sitting down. You need to hear me for once. Do you understand me? Don't listen to me... HEAR ME!!" she snapped back.

Levi took in what she said before he sat down on the couch and stared at her. She knew he was in disbelief at the way she'd spoken to him since she's never said anything back to him before or went against anything he wanted her to do. Ariana was showing him a completely different side of her for once that made her proud of herself. Now only if she could stand up to her parents the way she just stood up to Levi, that would've made everything about their situation better, in her mind. Standing there fuming, Ariana realized it was time to tell Levi the real reason she didn't deal with her parents.

Sighing, she took a seat next to him on the couch. He looked her upside her head and waited for her to speak. Taking a minute to gather her thoughts, inhaling and exhaling, she knew this was going to be hard. With their relationship barely hanging on she didn't want to say anything that could destroy it.

"I'm sorry for yelling at you and I'm sorry for nagging, but you have to understand things from my point of view. You don't know the things I've gone through in my life or the reason I chose not to talk to my family. You don't know my life, so you can't judge me."

"Judge you? When have I ever judged you? You know so much about me and all the wrongs I've done both in the past and now, so who am I to judge anybody?"

"Don't do that."

"Don't do what?"

"You know what you're doing. You try to play this innocent role every time we have a problem. You try to put it all on me and make it seem like you're the victim, but that's not going to happen this time. You're going to have to man up and take responsibility for all the wrong you've done within our relationship too. This isn't all on me."

"I never said anything about this being all on you or being all your fault. I know I've had my fair share of mess ups, but I'm not going to sit here and allow you to make like you're innocent either."

The room fell silent. Neither of them realized that while they were going back and forth trying to play the blame game, they still looked away from the bigger picture, Ariana was pregnant. After they sat in the room silent for several minutes, Levi stood from his seat.

"So, you just gonna get rid of my seed without considering my feelings?"

"I never said that's what I was going to do. However, I am going to take my time and decide on what's best for me. Yeah, you did help create this situation we're currently in, but you aren't the one that's going to have to carry it. It's not your body that's about to get messed up. And, it's always easy for a man to walk away, but it's never the same case for a woman. I'm not going to allow you to be someone that comes in and out of our lives as you please. If you're doing it to me now, then I know you'll do it when the baby comes."

Levi walked up on Ariana. He had a look on his face that she's never seen and couldn't read. The expression on his face wasn't a pleasant one to her either. A sense of fear came over her, but she knew that she didn't need to do anything too drastic or move too fast because she was worried that he'd hurt her. At that moment, he wasn't the man that she'd fallen in love with. He was the man that she didn't want to be near any longer and that she was fearful would only cause more problems in her life. She wanted the Leviticus back that she met two years ago. She wanted the man back that could make her body melt at just the slightest touch. She didn't know how she was going to do that, especially with the anger she'd caused him by keeping such a big secret from him.

"I'm sorry," she sincerely apologized.

"I don't care," he hissed. "The day you think I'm going to allow you to kill my seed is the day that you are dead to me. You better think long and hard about your decision because your next move could be your last move," he warned her before he pushed passed her and out the door.

Ariana flopped down on her couch to get her thoughts together. She knew that something had to give if she wanted things to turn around for her. Knowing whatever changes needed to be made were going to have to start with her. She picked up her phone preparing herself for that long overdue conversation that needed to be had.

Chapter Six:

Esther

"It's so good to see you here tonight, Sister Esther," Pastor Evans told Esther.

They were having revival at Mt. Sinai Missionary Baptist Church and she decided she would attend the service since it'd been a while since she'd been to church.

"Thank you. I'm shocked to be here as well. It's been a while since I've been in here," Esther replied as she looked around to survey the church and the people there. There were a lot of new faces and very little familiar faces. Esther wasn't mad that there weren't many people there that she knew because she knew it had been a while since she stepped foot inside of that church.

"Yes, it has really been a long time. How have you been? How are those children of yours?"

"They're good, I reckon. They don't keep in touch with me the way that they should," Esther informed him, even though she didn't feel right telling her business to the pastor.

"What do you think the reason is behind that?"

"They are still hurt behind what happened with Ruth and I can't say that I blame them. That's the reason that I've been straying away from church. It's not like I turned away from my belief in God, but I do question some of the decisions He's made pertaining to my life lately."

"What do you mean? Can you elaborate on that a little more for me?"

"I mean I can, but it won't benefit me from talking about it. Let's just move on with the service."

"It won't hurt you to talk about it, so when the service is over, I'd like for you to hang back, so we can talk about this a little further."

"Alight," Esther replied with a fake smile. She wasn't interested in talking to the pastor or anyone else about what had been going on with her personally. In fact, she almost made up in her mind that she wanted to sneak out the back door instead of sitting through the service. At least then, she wouldn't have to worry about the pastor looking for her trying to talk after church was over.

"Hey First Lady Evans! Do you mind sitting next to Sister Esther during the service? I want to make sure she's able to follow what I say and if she has any questions, she can look to you for clarification and guidance," the pastor told his wife. Esther stood there looking crazy. She felt like Pastor Evans was practically getting his wife to babysit her and she wasn't about to go for that. She was a grown woman and knew how to find him if she wanted to talk to him.

"Oh, you don't have to do that. I have my Bible and it translates anything that I have difficulty understanding."

The pastor opened his mouth to say something, but Esther didn't want to hear anything more he had to say. She hated to be disobedient or even disrespectful to one of God's servants, but she was not about to allow the pastor or anyone else to pressure her into something that she didn't want to do.

"Sister Esther! Sister Esther! Can I speak with you briefly?" One of the church members jogged up behind her.

Esther stopped in her tracks and then turned around with her hands on her hip. She wasn't interested in hiding her attitude because she was tired of everyone stopping her when all she wanted to do was to get to her seat and enjoy the service.

"This is the reason I've been avoiding coming to church," Esther stated, even though she thought she'd said it to where she only she could hear.

"Oh, wow. I thought it was because you were still shaken up about what happened to Ruth. I really came over here to check on you, but if it's a problem, then I'll make sure I won't check on you again."

"I'm sorry, Brother Earl. It's been a lot for me to deal with lately and I'm constantly worried about the boys since they've been in Chicago. You know it's not one of the top places to live with all the violence. And with us being from this small state and having different cultures than those people who live in Chicago, it makes me worry more about how my children have managed to fit in."

"Actually, I have a niece that attends that school. She told me that she sees Levi and Zech quite a bit."

"Oh really? Well, how are they doing? I try to talk to them as much as I can, but sometimes they make it difficult for me to do."

"Yeah. She told me that the boys have been around the campus a lot. Well, their names have and that they may be involved in some illegal activity."

"Not my boys. They don't even have a bad bone in their body. Well, I take that back. They may have their moments of being disrespectful or even questioning some of the things that God has done, but to do something that would get them put in jail... I don't see them doing it."

"You don't see it because it's your boys, but I'm telling you this before something happens. My niece doesn't lie, and she doesn't know Levi and Zech enough to make up stories on them, so you may want to look into the information I just gave you. Until then, I'll continue to talk to my niece to see what other information I can dig up and I'll let you know what I find." Immediately, worry took over Esther. She knew that her children struggled with getting over their sister's death, but there was no reason for her boys to do anything that could get them arrested.

The whole time Esther sat in the service thinking about what Brother Earl had said to her, she knew that she needed to do something. She stepped out of the service to go to the parsonage of the church and pulled out her cell phone to call both boys. Neither of them answered the phone, but she left a message for them to call her. Because she was so used to calling the boys and neither of them answering the phone, she didn't let it bother her. She'd done it several times and as usual, they always pop up to talk to her only when they need something or want her to pray for them.

Esther left a message on both of the boy's voicemail asking that they return her call. She prayed that she wasn't making the calls in vain because they barely ever called or texted to check on her or to just talk to her and see how she was doing.

"Oh wait... I didn't try to call Ruth," she said to herself. Just that quick, she'd forgotten that Ruth was dead.

Dialing Ruth's number, the phone rung three times before going to voicemail. Ruth's phone was different from the boys because hers at least had a greeting before it beeped for her to be able to leave a message.

"You've reached the right person, at the wrong time. Leave a message and I might call you back," is what the message said, followed by a giggle and then the beep.

"That don't sound nothing like my Ruth," Esther snarled and then tried to call the number again. Nothing was different when she called this time... the phone went to voicemail again.

Esther listened to the message once again and then proceeded to leave a message.

"Hey Baby Girl, this is your mother. Have you checked on your brothers lately? I tried to call them, and they didn't answer. I know they won't call me back, but I know they'd never avoid your call. Please call me back. I love you and want to make sure you're okay, too."

"Who you talking to?" Brother Earl walked up on Esther to see who she was on the phone with. Esther jumped because she wasn't expecting anyone to be in the parsonage with her.

"What are you doing back here?"

"I'm just checking to make sure you're okay."

"I'm fine. I called my children to make sure they were okay. The boys never answer the phone, but I thought for sure that Ruth would."

"Ruth?"

"Yes, Ruth; my daughter. I know they haven't been to church in a while, but you should remember all of my babies." Brother Earl looked on, not knowing what to say to her. He didn't want to make her feel uncomfortable and he surely didn't want to be the one that had to remind her that Ruth had died.

"I'll be right back," he told her before marching back inside the church. He went in search of the pastor and didn't care if he had to pull him from the pulpit to get him to come out and talk to Esther. He felt that she was having a mental break and he didn't want to be the one to tell her.

It wasn't long before half the congregation was back in the parsonage with Esther attempting to make sure she was okay. By the time they'd reached her, she was on the floor holding a bear that she'd taken out of the children's Sunday school room. She cradled the bear as if she were holding an actual person.

"Esther, come on and get up. We need to go get you some help."

"I'm fine. We don't need to go get anything," Esther grimaced.

"Esther, Ruth is gone. You have to let her go in order to begin the healing process," Pastor Evans pleaded with her.

"I just called her phone and left her a message. She'll call me back."

Esther did indeed call Ruth's phone and heard the greeting that Ruth put on it right before she was killed. Levi and Zech made it a point to pay her phone bill each month to keep it on. That was the only way they'd be able to hear her voice and talk to her when they needed someone to talk to. When her voicemail was full, one of them would go in and clear out all of the messages so they could fill it up again.

"Call an ambulance," the First Lady spoke to one of the ushers. "She's got to get help."

That was the best thing they could do for Esther. She'd avoided being around others unless she was gone to work and even then, she often thought she'd seen Ruth or heard her voice. She was clearly displaying signs of post-traumatic stress mixed with depression and if she didn't get help soon, she wouldn't be any good to herself or anyone else.

Chapter Seven:

Zechariah

When the brothers parted ways, things were still not sitting right with Zech. He wanted to prove to his brother that his intuition was right about Amp. Yeah, he'd hooked them up with a lot of their hits, but he also showed signs of shadiness, and he was too big on loyalty to let that slide.

Taking an Uber back to Amp's house, he had them drop him off around the corner, so nobody would see him coming. He'd been to Amp's house on more than enough occasions to know how to get in and out, undetected. He also knew how to go through the secret tunnel that connected Amp's house to the house next door. That was the route he chose to take that night. He didn't want Amp or anyone else to be warned when he appeared because he was about to show everybody that he was not the one to screw over.

After exiting the Uber, Zech surveyed his surroundings before walking through the yard of the house behind Amp's, then jumping the fence. Amp had two bulldogs chained up in his backyard, that alerted him when there was an intruder. Zech wasn't worried about the dogs barking because he'd been around them long enough for them to learn him. Plus, he figured out ways to get them to shut up.

When he was near the dogs, they became excited and started jumping around and whimpering.

"Hey Cajon and Spike. I know you happy to see me. How have my babies been?" Zech somewhat got caught up in the moment and began baby talking the dogs. He did that often to them, so that wasn't anything new for any of them.

Zech played with them for a minute and then he opened two beef jerkies and gave each of them one before he sidestepped to the vacant house next door. He made sure to continue to scope out the scene and move slowly so he wouldn't be caught off guard. Going through the back door, he headed straight for the basement door. He had to use the light on his cell phone to illuminate a path for him, but he didn't turn on the flashlight because he didn't want to give off too much light.

Very slowly, he made his way through the basement, crossing the path that ran from the vacant house's basement to Amp's basement. He could hear Amp in there entertaining someone. The voice sounded like Jaclyn, but he wasn't too sure and certainly wasn't about to jump out and confront them without affirmation. Quietly, he stood in the same spot waiting for confirmation that it was indeed her.

"Then you saw how Zech tried to go for Mia? She don't want his retarded ass," Jaclyn cracked. It pissed Zech off when he heard Jaclyn and Amp talk about him the way that they did, but he remained calm. After he was sure that he was correct about who Amp was with, it caused him to smirk.

"He tried to play tough in front of us like he didn't want her when he knew he wanted that dusty cat this whole time," he whispered to himself.

Zech rested in the same spot for well over ten minutes trying to listen to what Amp and Jaclyn were talking about. He wanted to see if Amp would say anything that would verify all the negative thoughts he had about him.

"So, you think they got them?"

"I sure hope so. I was getting tired of those lil niggas anyway. They whined too much about little petty shit," Amp laughed. Jaclyn joined in along with him.

"I'm not gon' lie tho. I would've given' Levi a test ride. He looks like he can put it down in the bedroom."

"Naw. That quiet one is the one you need to worry about; those are the ones that'll blow your back out."

Zech was appalled at what he'd heard. He couldn't believe that Amp had just referred to him in a sexual manner, but he still never revealed his presence. Silent he remained as he waited to see how the conversation was going to conclude.

"You still get down like that? I thought you were good off women."

"Don't play me, Jaclyn. You know if it ain't about the cat, then I don't get down like that. I was just telling you that people say the quiet ones are the ones for you to watch." A sense of relief fell upon Zechariah. He wouldn't be able to look at Amp the same again if he knew that he was checking him out.

"Oh, I got you. But, let me get up out of here. When will we know if the police picked them up?"

"I'm waiting for my potna' that I got working at the police station to call me now. They should've been picked up at least a few hours ago. They're probably just processing them in or something."

"And you're cool with setting them up like that?"

"Look, the heat was starting to come down on me. There was no way I was about to go down, so I put it on them. Hell, that's the cost you pay to be the boss."

"But you're the boss," Jaclyn call herself correcting him.

"Shut up! I know I'm the boss, but they gon' have to take the fall for this one. I have way more to lose than they do."

"How? They're the ones in school. They have a mother that loves them. You know this will tear her apart," Jaclyn tried to reason with him.

"Who the hell are you to come in my crib and try to correct me about something I did? I said they were taking the fall and I meant that. Matter fact, get your ass out my shit. You not bout to come in here and challenge my decisions. I don't care about them or they nappy headed mammie."

Just as Amp stood up to escort Jaclyn out of his house, they were bomb rushed by a bunch of men that Zech had never seen before; or so he thought. There had to be a total of five men standing around in the room with Jaclyn and Amp. He squinted his eyes hoping to get a better view of the different men. Two of them, he could've sworn he'd seen before. They reminded him of two of men that went out with him, his brother, and Amp on one of the very first hits that they pulled.

"What the-?" Before Amp could finish his statement, he was punched in the mouth.

"Shut up, Punk. Where the money at?"

"What money?"

"Don't try me. I'll blow her brains out all on your floor."

"I don't care about that broad. I don't know her like that; kill that hoe if you want."

Jaclyn screamed out in fear at the way Amp practically sacrificed her to save himself. Zech was outdone at the way that Amp bitched up twice in one day. He'd never seen a man so weak in his life. The sad part was that they thought Amp was big on loyalty, but he'd just showed Zech how quick he forgot about loyalty when it came down to saving himself.

"Shut that broad up," one of the men stated.

Pow... Pow... Pow...

Without a second thought, the man that was holding Jaclyn, let three rounds out in her head. Her body dropped to the floor faster than a speeding bullet.

"You next. Now, tell me where the money is. I'm not gon' be so nice the next time."

"Come on, Puncho. You know I ain't got money like that. Levi and Zech gon' to make a hit right now. They should be back any minute." Hearing Amp say Puncho's name confirmed that he was one of the men that went out with them. What he didn't understand was why Puncho would want to rob Amp? If they were as close as they claimed to be when he first met them, then just like he did, Puncho should've known where Amp kept his money. Since Amp was doing his best not to talk, Zech felt a little better because he knew he was about to have a big come up.

Amp continued to lie like he didn't have any money at his house. It wasn't a lie he didn't keep the money in his house. Puncho frowned at Amp as if he knew he were lying too, before he repeatedly sent blow after blow to

Amp's head. He bellowed over in pain trying to cover his body from the plows being inflicted on him.

"Puncho, chill out. Levi and Zech out makin' a hit now. As soon as I get the money off it, I'll cut you in on it," Amp chided before spitting blood from his mouth.

"You must take me for a fool."

"No man. You're like a brother to me. I'm telling the truth, man."

"Check this clown out. He thinks I'm stupid as hell or something for real. How the hell is Levi out getting money with his brother when I just saw him over by his girl's house?" Amp's eyes grew as wide as a deer caught in headlights. He thought he had everything all figured out but didn't bank on what would happen if Levi and Zech didn't get arrested.

"Handle this fool while I search the house."

Zech stood there the whole time with his phone on record. He'd taken it out the moment he heard Amp on the couch talking to Jaclyn, everything needed to prove Amp set them up recorded. He also caught everything about the men jumping on Amp. He knew his time was limited when they decided they were going to tear the place up looking for the money. Zech knew where the money was hidden. He was not about to let someone walk away with what he thought was owed to him. Taking his phone off record mode, switching to the camera he wasted no time taking individual pics of the five men that were standing over Jaclyn's lifeless body and even did a small recording to get everything that was surrounding the room in case he needed any evidence to free himself. When he had everything, he thought he'd need, he swiftly turned around and headed back the way he'd gone in.

Inside the abandoned house, Zech marched straight back to the room that was considered to be the master bedroom. Moving quickly, he walked straight to the back of the walk-in closet. Pulling down on the rod used to hang the clothes, he was able to open a secret door where Amp stored all of his money and things he could not get rid of that they'd taken from people's homes. There were two large duffle bags filled with money inside. Zech grabbed both bags and closed the secret door back. If he needed to, he'd go back for the items that they couldn't get rid of. Knowing that he didn't have a ride of his own, he didn't want to move anything that would set off red flags. He pulled out his phone and went to his Uber app.

Putting in the address where he was dropped off, he left out the house like he owned it and headed back to his original destination.

As Zech was passing the dogs, they began to bark loudly. He wondered why they didn't bark when the other group of men showed up, but then he remembered that two of those men had been around those dogs before. Zech heard something behind him and picked up his pace.

"Aye, who's back there?" someone called out.

Zech became nervous and did the only thing he could think to do, which was to run. Not one time did he think about dropping the bags that he carried. He ran like his life depended on it as someone was chasing behind him. When he rounded the front yard, he saw that his Uber driver was out there. The driver saw him and got out the car.

"Don't get your dumb ass out. Punch the gas as soon as I get in," Zech ordered.

Scared of what was going on, the driver wasted no time putting the pedal to the metal when he noticed that Zech had completely gotten in.

"What's going on?" the man turned around to ask.

"Denali? Is that your name?"

"Yes, why?"

"If you don't turn around and mind your business, you won't have to worry about my business or anyone else's because I'ma permanently shut your mouth." Doing as he was told, Denali shut his mouth and focused on getting to his destination because had a wife and three kids at home.

Zech recovered his phone from his back pocket and immediately punched in his brother's number.

"Sup?" Levi answered on the second ring and appeared to be agitated.

"What's up with you?"

"Ariana's ass bout to make me mess her up. What's up tho?"

"I'm headed to the room. You need to be there when I get there. You won't believe what I have to tell you," Zech blurted out and then ended the call without giving his brother the chance to respond.

On the entire ride back to the dorm, Zech thought over and over in his head about the events of the night. He wished like hell he could've been the one to put a bullet in

Amp's head or at least been able to stay around to see the other men handle him, but he knew that wouldn't have been wise for him.

"I hope this fool believes me now," Zech said to himself as he rested his head on the back of the seat.

All he wanted was to make enough money to pay for school, so he wouldn't have to take out any loans. To buy or do whatever he wanted to do, when he wanted, ; and to take care of his mother even though he wasn't dealing with her too tough after everything that happened with his sister. He figured the money he'd coped from Amp would be enough to give him a head start on the things he wanted to do for himself; he also knew he was still going to have to do at least three more big hits to live comfortably without any worries. Well, not worry while he was still in school.

Chapter Eight:

Leviticus

Levi paced back and forth in the dorm, thinking about what had just transpired between Ariana and himself. He couldn't believe she was considering getting rid of his baby without even talking to him about it first. That meant she didn't trust his abilities to love her and be responsible enough to be there for both her and their unborn child.

Zech opening the door while Levi was in deep thought caught him off guard. Levi instantly pulled his nine out of his waistband as a protective measure.

"Aye man, what you doing?" Zech squealed with his hands raised up in the air. He dropped both of the bags he'd carried in with him.

"You scared the hell out of me. You could've warned me that you were coming."

"If I told you to meet me here, how could you not know I was coming? What's going on with you? Why are you sweating like that? And where the hell did you get a gun from?"

"Ariana's pregnant!" Levi blurted out, completely overlooking the rest of the questions that Zech had asked him. Saying it aloud to someone else caused him to feel nauseous. *How could I be so careless*, he thought to himself.

"Say what?"

"You heard me. She's pregnant."

"Is that good or bad?" Zech honestly inquired. Levi had never talked about wanting children before, so it wasn't farfetched that someone would want to know if he would be happy being a father.

"What you mean? How could that be a good thing when I can't even take care of myself? Do I look like I'm ready to be somebody's father?"

"Calm down, fool. You sitting over there crying about being a father, but yet you didn't do anything to prevent the pregnancy."

"I was more than careful," Levi spoke with a raised voice. "We used condoms and she was on birth control," he continued.

"And neither of those methods are one hundred percent effective. If you didn't want any kids, you should've kept your lil friend to yourself," Zech teased, trying to make light of the situation, but Levi wasn't having it.

"Shut the hell up. You starting to sound like your mother," Levi acknowledged.

"Is that right?"

"Don't go there with me, ZECHARIAH," he raised his voice to show how serious he was. "You know how I feel about having baby's outside of wedlock. Hell, I don't even know if Ariana's the one for me. She nags and she's too independent for me. What man wants a woman that doesn't know that the man is supposed to be the head of the household?"

"Well LEVITICUS, you're saying all of that, but that's another one of those times where you have to question if you've done anything to show her signs that you are ready to lead her."

"I knew I shouldn't have said anything to you about this because you're always passing judgment on folks and I don't need that. I need my brother right now, more than ever," Levi mumbled.

"I'm being your brother, but I'm also not going to tell you something just because it's something you want to hear. You need to know the truth. That's the only way you'll be able to grow from this situation."

"I'm good. What did you need to talk to me about?" Levi attempted to change the subject. He didn't want to hear Zech lecture him about anything else because he knew his temper was short and he didn't want to say anything that would cause him to look bad in his brother's eyes when he knew all Zech had tried to do was help. He was the reason behind his demise and early loss of freedom that'll happen when the baby shows up.

"I needed to talk to you about Amp, but I'm not sure if I should tell you about it now considering what you're going through. You just changed the subject, so I know there's more to the story that you haven't told me. I'm pretty sure the anger that you're displaying right now has nothing to do with the fact that she's pregnant, but the thought that you're going to have to give up being able to do what you want to do and start doing what's right, including being the father your child needs. You know...the father we never had."

"Again... What did you need to talk to me about?"

"Fine, but we will talk about this again."

"Not if I have anything to do with it."

"Trust and believe me, we will. And if you don't, then when I call and talk to ma, you're going to have a lot of explaining to do." That was Zech's way of threatening Levi that if he didn't talk to him, he was going to call and tell their mother everything that was going on.

"You so cold-blooded."

"I learned from the best," Zech returned, sticking his tongue out at his brother.

"I hate yo ass," Levi refuted before running towards his brother.

They began tussling and wrestling with each other like they used to do when they were younger. It was something they both needed. Zech needed it to let go of some of the anger he felt towards the way Amp had tried to set him and his brother up. Levi needed it to let go of the ill-feelings he had towards Ariana and not knowing what she was going to do about his unborn child.

The playful interaction between them went on for roughly ten minutes. By that time, both boys were out of breath and wanted to get some things off their chest.

"I'm sorry, man. I shouldn't have been taking my anger out on you. I'm pissed that Ariana doesn't know what she's going to do with the baby and it's driving me crazy. You wanna know the worse part of that?"

"What's that?"

"I've been knowing she was pregnant for a while now, but I never said anything because I was waiting for her to share the news with me. Well, when she pissed me off yesterday, that's when I started blurting out everything that I knew. That wasn't the best time for me to be saying anything, but I couldn't help it. All types of emotions were running through me, and I was sick of her always fussing at me about things and actin like she's perfect."

"Wow, that's bad, bruh," Zech sarcastically stated. Levi eyeballed him and prepared to say something out of line, but Zech stopped him when he opened his mouth to speak again. "It'll be okay, Levi. I know it seems bad now, but once you talk to Ariana, things will be okay. I'm sure all she wants is to be reassured that you'll be there for her.

That'll play a big part in what decision she makes about the baby. I'm here if you need me and I don't mind talking to her for you. Just let me know what you want me to do, I got you."

"Thanks, man, I needed that," Levi confessed. He stood up off the floor that they'd fallen on while they were wrestling and started to go over to his bed until he tripped and fell on top of one of the duffle bags. "The hell?"

"Yeah... That's what I needed to talk to you about."

"What you mean? Did I miss something?"

"You may want to sit down for this one," Zech warned. Levi looked up at him like he was worried. Zech nodded his head towards the bed to tell Levi to sit down again.

"Why do I feel like I'm going to have a headache by the time you're done talking?"

"Oh, trust me, you're going to have wayyyyyy more than a headache," Zech assured him.

After taking a seat on his bed, Levi began massaging his temples. He knew Zech had a problem with Amp and he wished that he'd let whatever the issue he had go. Levi was not prepared for the information that his brother was about to hit him with.

"First, I need you to have an open mind about this because this is the only way you'll be able to see Amp's true colors."

"Will you let this little vendetta you have against him go? I don't have time to keep listening to you and him, go back and forth with each other like little children that don't want to share a toy."

"And I get tired of my brother playing me for a nigga he met just a few years ago. I've known you since you came out the cat. If you gonna continue to take up for this clown over me, then you might as well let him be your brother." Zech rose to his feet once he'd given Levi an ultimatum.

"Take your panties out of your ass. It's not that serious."

"It is that serious. You're my brother, and you're supposed to remain loyal to me, but you're too busy munchin' on that nigga's balls to see what's been in your face this entire time."

"I'm not munchin' on a damn thing. You better watch how you talking to me or else..."

"Or else what? Ain't nobody scared of your punk ass," Zech fumed. He made his way towards his brother.

"I'm telling you that you're about to get a beating that you're not prepared for. You better get out my face."

"Naw, you're the one about to get the beating. It's all good though because you not worth the trouble. I was being the brother I was taught to be and coming in to stop you from making what could be an even bigger mistake by continuing to try to work with Amp, but I'm done. Fuck him and fuck you!" Zech grabbed both of the duffle bags full of money and left out the room.

"Punk ass!" Levi yelled behind the door. He didn't know if he should've been madder at himself or his brother. To him, Amp had been more than loyal, and nobody produced anything that showed him otherwise, so why was Zech all of a sudden against him?

Levi figured that somewhere along the way, Zech grew jealous of the relationship he'd developed with Amp and therefore, he was doing any and everything that he could to break that bond. However, Levi was not about to let that happen. Amp had given them an opportunity and chance to make money when no one else did. There was no way he could turn his back on the one person he felt remained down with him.

Chapter Nine:

Esther

"How are you today, Ms. Jeffries?"

"I'm as good as good can be. How may I help you?"

"Do you know why you're here?"

"Yeah. Because the people at the church were nosey as hell and thought I needed to be checked out. There's nothing wrong with me and I'd like to go home."

"I understand that you feel there's nothing wrong, but you had a serious episode last night where you were hallucinating," Doctor Jenkins attempted to explain to Esther.

"I don't care what you thought I had, but I was perfectly fine and I'm not staying here, so you might as well go ahead and get my discharge papers."

"You know that I have to tell you that you don't need to be leaving at a time like this. I'd like for you to at least talk to our psychiatrist to make sure you don't need to change your medication or there is something more we can do for you."

"The only thing you can do for me is allow me to go home. I know I'll have to leave against medical advice (AMA), but I don't care. I don't want to be here. I don't need your help or anybody else's," she refuted.

"Yes, you would be considered leaving AMA, but we can't make you stay anywhere you don't want to be. Are you sure that you don't at least want to talk to the psychiatrist first?"

"Will it make you shut up with all the questions and allow me to leave?"

"You'd still be leaving AMA, unless Dr. Rester say that you're okay to leave."

"Fine, that'll be a piece of cake," Esther sassed. "Go ahead and get him."

Doctor Jenkins stepped out the room in search of Dr. Rester. Esther remained in her bed staring out the window as she'd done the whole time she'd been admitted. It was roughly forty-five minutes later, before Dr. Rester showed up to evaluate her. Because of his tardiness, Esther already had an attitude and already had it made up in her mind that she was not going to be receptive to him and anything he had to say to her.

"Good afternoon, Ms. Jeffries."

"Call me Esther."

"Well, Esther... I'm Dr. Rester. Do you know why we had to admit you to the hospital?"

"Because I went to church last night and almost had to set it off in there. The congregation felt like something was wrong with me because they'd never seen that side of me before and instead of telling me to go home, they decided to be a bunch of buttholes and call an ambulance on me."

"Esther, who is Ruth?"

"Ruth is my daughter, why?"

"You were holding a teddy bear claiming that it was Ruth."

"And? What does that have to do with anything?" Esther didn't see a problem with her behavior because it was something she'd done before while she was at home. She knew that Ruth was dead, but there were times when she felt like Ruth was amongst her.

"Where is Ruth now?"

"Ruth is with God."

"So, you do know that she is dead?"

"How could I not know that she's dead when I was there when she took her last breath?" Dr. Rester sat in silence observing Esther and her movements. He knew that nothing he could say to Esther would make the situation better. He also could tell that she wasn't interested in being there, which wasn't a good thing. If she wasn't going to be open and honest through her talk with him, then there was basically nothing he could do for her.

"Is there anything you'd like to talk to me about?"

"Yeah... Dr. Jenkins said I could go home after talking to you. All I want to do is be released. There ain't nothing ya'll can do for me because I don't need any help."

"Okay... I'm sorry that you feel that way. But, I'm going to give you my card."

"For what?"

"In case you need to talk. My cell phone number is on there as well and I'm accessible pretty much any time."

"Yeah. Thanks!"

Dr. Rester stood up to leave the room. He halted by the door for a few minutes to see if she'd possibly stop him and want to talk. After three minutes of standing there, he left out the room in search of Dr. Jenkins.

It wasn't long before a nurse walked inside the room with paperwork for Esther to be discharged. The nurse was quiet the entire time she was in the room with Esther which made her a little jittery. She wasn't used to medical staff being quiet when they walked in to see her.

"What's the problem?"

"Excuse me?"

"I asked what the problem was. Why are you so quiet?"

"Well, they said you didn't want to talk to anybody and I don't want to go against your wishes."

"What do you have to say? Everyone else has had something to say about me being here, so why not join in with them?"

"When I say self-love, self-respect, and self-worth to you, what do they have in common?"

"That they are things people need to have in their lives," Esther cooed.

"They are all things that you can't get from other people. You have to love yourself, respect yourself, and know your worth. When you came in here last night and even by the way that you've acted today, it is clear that you don't have those attributes. Talking to Dr. Rester doesn't mean that you're crazy, it just means that you have a lot going on and need someone to talk to that won't judge you."

"What makes you think you know me?"

"I've been where you are."

"You've never been where I'm at. You don't know what it's like to lose a child," Esther shouted.

"I've lost three children.... One I miscarried, the second one lived three days, and the other one died at the age of five. No, they weren't killed, but they were still children that I loved and needed in my life, so don't tell me what I've been through."

Esther felt stupid for the way she'd spoken to the nurse. She'd done the one thing she didn't want people to do to her and that was to judge her. She listened to the nurse tell her story and how she felt better after she talked to someone outside of her normal family and friends. Esther could then see how that would make a bit of a difference.

They talked for close to an hour and Esther enjoyed the conversation. She knew the nurse could've gotten in trouble for sitting in her room for so long, but Esther would've covered for her because she really needed the conversation they had. By the time the nurse was prepared to leave her room, Esther told her that she would see someone, but it would be when she was released home. The nurse let her know that she understood that and went and got Dr. Rester so that he could set some appointments up with Esther. They'd rather her leave with the intentions of coming back to get help, then to leave and not care about getting help at all.

Chapter Ten:

Zechariah

Zech was furious at the way his brother treated him over someone that wasn't even blood related to them. He wanted so badly to punch Levi's face in, but he didn't want to hurt his mother. They were the only children she had left, and although she hadn't been doing well since their sister's death, they knew she still loved them, and it would tear her up if her sons were not getting along with one another.

When Zech left the dorms, he went to The Pub. He had a friend that worked there and would let him drink even though he wasn't old enough to do so. He must've been sitting at the bar for about twenty minutes before someone came prancing over towards him.

"Is it okay if I take a seat?" the female voice inquired. When Zech looked up, he smiled at the sight before him.

"You sure you want to be sitting here with me? I mean you did think I was only trying to get between your legs."

"Let's be real... You and I both know you want some of this," she freely spoke before pointing at her vaginal area.

"At some point, I plan on getting it, but not off the bat. Hell, for all I know, you could have the heebie-jeebies," he cracked.

"Naw boo, I'm cleaner than the board of health over here. You can try that with someone else."

"I hear ya. Gon' take a seat," Zech informed her. He wanted to be alone, but he figured she'd stand over him and he'd preferred she sat down.

Mia made herself comfortable sitting down next to Zech. This is quite cozy," she expressed, trying to make small talk.

"It's cool."

"You don't want to talk? What's wrong with you?"

"It's a long story that I don't care to talk about," Zech explained. Realistically, it would've been nice if he had someone to talk to about his problems, but he didn't trust people outside of his immediate family.

"Come on, Zech; I thought we were better than that."

"After the way you tried to clown me earlier, we ain't better than shit," he angrily spat, while slurring a little from the two shots of Hennessey he'd consumed since walking through the door.

"I know what you need," Mia seductively whispered in his ear before grabbing his wrist and trying to pull him behind her.

"Where you taking me?"

"Just shut up and come on," she sassed and continued to pull him behind her.

Mia pulled Zech by the arm until they reached the hallway where the bathrooms were located. She surveyed the hall to make sure no one was watching before she knocked on the women's door. Not getting an answer, she slowly turned the knob to peek inside. Finding it empty, she yanked Zech's arm in one swift motion and pulled him into the bathroom behind her before closing and locking the door.

"What the hell are you doing?" Zech asked while licking his lips.

"It ain't that kind of party. I'm just trying to make you feel better." She reached into her bra and pulled out a bag with three blunts that were already rolled up.

"Damn... I didn't think you got down like that."

"There's a lot people don't know about me. But, I take it all with a grain of salt and keep doing me. I learned a long time ago you can't let everybody in on everything you do and that's the main reason I've been able to keep things about me as quiet as they've been. Ask anybody on campus about me, even Jaclyn, and I bet most of them won't even be able to tell you my last name."

Mia continued to talk as Zech took a seat on the toilet. Mia made sure two of the blunts were wrapped securely before she lit them and handed one to Zech. Immediately, Zech began to profusely cough when he exhaled. It'd been a while since he smoked anything, so it damn near knocked the wind out of him.

"Slow down, chocker. I don't need you dying on my watch," Mia joked.

"Man, what's in this?"

"Nothing that you should be concerned about. Now, tell me what's bothering you," Mia instructed as she pushed Zech back on the toilet seat and straddled him.

Zech had all types of thoughts running through his mind. He wanted Mia in the worse way. Mia didn't make the situation any better as she leaned in and began placing kisses on his neck. Not able to control himself any longer, Zech put the blunt out, and in one swift motion, Mia was no longer in her shirt. She tried to protest, but before the words could leave her mouth, he'd quickly unfasted her bra freeing her breast from total confinement. Throwing her head back, she was lost in the pleasure she was receiving from him.

Sucking and pinching, pinching and sucking eyes rolling back, and her breath caught in her throat as she stumbled over her words

"Oh, ooohh my Goddddd…. Wha.. what are you doing to me?" Mia belched out. Zech didn't answer.

A few minutes later, he lifted her up and carried her to the nearest wall. Placing her back up against it, he worked quickly to pull down his pants and boxers to unleash the beast that had grown rapidly in his pants. Glad she was in a skirt, his hands found the thin string holding her together, ripped them off, and inserted his stiff rod inside of her hot and wet honey pot. Slowly, he glided in and out of her; the wetness was like music to his ears. The feeling he was experiencing was one unfamiliar to him.

"Damn girl, you feel so good."

"Do I?"

"Hell yeah. You know I gotta make you mine after this."

"Oh really?" Mia questioned. Zech increased his pace and deepened his strokes being sure to hit her spot each time he plunged inside of her.

"Damnnnnnnnn…." she yelled out.

"What you say?" Zech asked, taunting her.

"What are you doing to me?" Mia inquired again.

"Don't worry about it, just enjoy it…"

Mia tried throwing her head back, but it bumped against the wall. She began to yell louder, but Zech placed his hand over her mouth to keep her from getting too loud. Zech tightened the grip he had on her to prevent her from moving. All she could do was take the beating he was putting on her, and she loved every minute of it.

Twenty minutes later they were leaning against the wall, panting and out of breath. Zech couldn't believe he'd had sex with Mia after she turned him down earlier.

"You good?"

"Yeah. I'm good. You good?"

"I'm better than good," Mia replied while walking over to the sink to soap some paper towels and clean herself up.

"Are you really doing that right now?"

"Yeah. We out and I'm not finna go around other people smelling like tuna tar-tar."

"Well, you were kinda smelling like that before I went in, so you going to need more than some hand soap to handle that," Zech teased.

Mia flipped him the bird and continued cleaning herself.

"You go out first," she instructed him, and he did just that. He opened the door and peeked outside to make sure no one was in the hall before he stepped out the bathroom. He walked next door to the men's restroom to clean himself up before he went to reclaim his seat at the bar.

It wasn't long before Mia rejoined Zech. He had a glass of Hennessey up to his mouth that she snatched from his hand. She swallowed the drink down in one gulp, and then picked his phone up.

"Unlock your phone."

"For what?"

"You wanted my number, didn't you?"

Zech didn't respond to her. Instead, he unlocked the phone and handed it back to her. Mia put her number in and then gave him the phone back and walked away. Zech didn't bother getting up to go after her. He told himself he'd hit her up in a few days, but he was going to spend the rest of his night drinking away his sorrow.

Chapter Eleven:

Ariana

Ariana tried her best to reach out to Levi, but he wouldn't answer her calls or respond to her text. She allowed three days to pass before she decided it was time that she went and got her man. She still didn't know what she wanted to do as far as the baby was concerned and made up in her mind that she wasn't going to be in a hurry to make a decision.

Ariana wore a maxi dress that was right above her knees and some cute strappy sandals to match. She didn't want to look too cute there, but she also wanted to show Levi what he'd be missing if he let her get away. Combing her wrap down, she checked herself one last time in the mirror before she grabbed her purse, phone, and keys and made her way out the door.

Inside her car, she turned the radio on to her favorite gospel station and began singing along with the music. Her walk with God is what she felt kept her sane. For some reason, she started thinking about the conversation she had with her father the night that Levi walked away from her.

"Hey Ana," he answered on the second ring.

"Hello, father. How have you been?"

"I've been worried sick about you. Why would you go off to school and not maintain contact with your family?"

"I have maintained contact with y'all. I just don't talk to you every day like I used to when I first got here," she explained.

"And why is that?"

"The older I got, the more I realize how wrong you were. You've done nothing but try to keep me away from dating black men or even having black friends when it's in my blood. I'm part African American and it seems like you want me to turn my back on my heritage."

"I never said you couldn't have black friends, but these men don't mean you any good."

"How do you know that?"

"Because I'm one and I know what it was like for me growing up. You think I'd tell you something if I didn't know for sure how it could break you."

"That's funny because momma gave you a chance," she raised her voice at him.

"Don't ever step out of your place with me. I'm your father and what I say goes."

"And that's the main reason I'm not coming home or maintaining contact with you. It's wrong of you to put black people in a box and think they will all do you wrong because of the way you've dealt with some in your past. You were young, those people were dumb, but you have allowed yourself to become just like them. Thinking so negatively about African American men, AND YOU'RE ONE."

"Ariana, what are you calling about? If you aren't dead or dying, then there is no reason for you to come at me with these shenanigans."

"I'm dating a black man, father."

"Well, as long as you're with him, then there's no reason for you to ever come back here."

"I'm pregnant by him as well. Are you saying that your grandchild can't come there either?" Her father was hesitant on the phone. The line grew silent, and Ariana took that as him trying to think of the right things to say.

"Like I said... If you're going to continue to date him and bring that nigger baby into this world, then you better not *ever return to this home. You are no longer apart of this family. I could care less what happens to you," her father roared before hanging the phone up on her.*

Ariana had never experienced that type of pain in her life. She didn't know if it would be worse to lose her father or lose Levi. Either way, she knew she'd be okay losing one but not the other and Levi was the one she wasn't willing to lose just yet.

Beep... Beep... Beep...

"Watch where you're driving, hoe!" an angry driver blew their horn at Ariana and screamed out obscenities when she veered over into their lane.

"I didn't try to you butterball shaped head ass idiot," she retorted before speeding past the car. It wasn't too much longer before she was pulling up on campus.

Ariana parked her car then headed towards the dorms. It wasn't a co-ed dorm, so to avoid security, she went to the back where no guard as in sight. She snuck in the door and headed up the stairs to Levi's room. Finally, after four knocks he responded.

"I knew you'd come bac-." he stopped himself from speaking when he realized that she wasn't who he thought it was.

"Expecting someone else?"

"I thought you were Zech. What the hell are you doing here?"

"I came to talk to you. I want us to be okay; I don't want to lose you."

"Get out of here, Ariana. I'm not ready to deal with you right now."

"How long are you going to think it's okay to talk to me like that? I'm the mother of your child!"

"Are you? You trying to get rid of my seed and ain't thought about talking to me about it."

"I never said that I was getting rid of the baby."

"No, what you said was that you hadn't decided what you were going to do yet. That's my baby too. I should have a say in it just as much as you do. I know it's your body, but if you don't want it, at least let me raise it," he suggested.

"God granted me the serenity to accept the things I cannot change; the courage to change the things that I can; and the wisdom to know the difference." Out of nowhere, Ariana started saying the *Serenity Prayer*.

"What are you even talking about right now?"

"As spiritual as your mother is, there ain't no way that you don't know that prayer."

"Don't bring my mother into this. She was a woman that kept three children." Levi fumed.

"I understand that you're mad at me, but that does not give you the right to talk to me any type of way. If you want to talk to me, then we can sit down like two adults and have a conversation and decide together what needs to happen. If not, then you need to tell me now, so I can go handle things the way I want to handle them."

Levi stood before Ariana making all types of expressions on his face but never saying a word. He didn't know what to say, didn't want to say the same thing. At that moment he didn't care about her feelings because he felt she didn't care about his.

"Levi, if you can promise me that you'll be there. I mean be present for this child and me, then I'll consider having it. I don't want to be a baby's momma. I want you to love and cherish me and make me your wife." Levi gulped like he'd been holding in a mouth full of water.

"Make you my wife? Who would marry a woman that they can't trust to come to them about a matter as serious as this?" he spat.

"I see that you're still mad, so I'm just going to leave this alone. But you need to know that I walked away from my family for you."

"Oh, I'm more than sure it wasn't for me, and if it was, I didn't ask you to walk away from anybody. You made that choice by yourself as you've seemingly been making all these other important choices by yourself. That shows you don't need a man because you're too busy trying to do what Ariana wants to do."

"That's not fair!!" she argued.

"Fair? You keep saying things aren't fair, but what have you done to make anything fair? What have you done to make this right for either of us?" Ariana stood there trying to fight back tears. "My point exactly."

"Fine. Get out!" she demanded.

"Get out? You in my shit!" he refuted.

Ariana observed the surroundings. It didn't take her long to figure out she was indeed in his dorm. *I'm tripping for real,* she thought to herself. In her mind, she knew she needed to get out of there, but her legs just wouldn't move. For some reason, she was scared to walk away and leave the man that she truly loved.

Chapter Twelve:

Leviticus

Levi could not figure out why Ariana was still in his room. He'd asked her nicely to get out, but she didn't get the point. If she wanted to get rid of is seed, then that meant she wanted to get rid of their relationship too. The fact that she told him that she walked away from her family for him didn't move him. He knew she was only doing it for herself.

"Why are you still here?"

"Because I love you, Levi. I'm sorry. Let's work this out; you're it for me, baby," Ariana pleaded, but again, Levi showed no ounce of care.

"Leave Ana. I'm not doing this with you. I have more important business to tend to."

"Like what? Going to steal something with Amp and your brother? You think I don't know what you do? You think I won't tell the police everything I know?"

"Quit playing with me, Ariana. You threatening me is only going to piss me off more. Don't press your luck with me."

"Oh, so you think I won't tell? Try me," Ariana warned as she pulled her phone for her purse. She began dialing numbers as if she were about to call the police, causing Levi to worry.

"Put the phone down."

"Why? You gonna talk to me now?"

"Yeah, let's talk." Levi's face twitched as he pulled out the chair in front of his desk and took a seat. Ariana followed suit by pulling out the chair from the other desk and sitting down. "Talk..."

"Where do you see us being in five years?"

"With the way you're acting now, I don't see us being anywhere. You threatening to call the police on me and you talking about getting rid of my baby, our baby; we would not be communicating at all."

"What if I don't get rid of the baby? Would you want to be with me then?"

"I can't be with you at all, Ariana. I love you true enough, but sometimes love isn't enough. You withheld information from me that I should've known from the jump and carried this burden by yourself when we were in a relationship and should've been working on this problem together. I can never forgive that."

"How did you find out anyway?"

"The day you took the test, I popped up over at your house. When I went to use the bathroom in the hallway I saw the test in the trashcan. I wanted to see if you were going to tell me, but you never opened your mouth and said a word. Why do you think I've been so distant and nonchalant about our relationship lately?"

"But why not just talk to me about it instead of holding on to a secret that would potentially change both of our lives?"

"Are you even listening to yourself? I waited for you to tell me. I thought you were going to surprise me by telling me, but the longer I waited for you to say something, the angrier I became," he insisted.

"Leviticus, you were too busy chasing behind Amp and creating these worthless crimes to worry about what was going on in our relationship. For months, I tried to tell you that something wasn't right with us and that we needed to spend more time together if we were going to make it, but you didn't care. You don't get how much I've sacrificed for this relationship."

"Why don't you tell me what you sacrificed? Tell me what's so big and important in your life that you gave it up to be with me?"

"MY FAMILY… I walked away from my family for you," the tears began to flow down her face relentlessly.

"I never asked you to give your family up for me. I don't even know anything about your family. I always thought maybe you were an orphan ward of the court or a foster child with no real family because you never even talked about introducing me to them."

"Listen, my father is completely against me being with a black man. They feel like all a black man will do is bring me down. I knew that taking you to meet my family would not turn out good, so I didn't do it. I should've been happy to take my man around my family, but that wasn't in the cards for me. I question God regularly about why my life was the way that it was."

"Don't do that."

"Don't do what?"

"Don't question God. It won't turn out good for you. No matter what you're going through or even the decisions you decide to make, what's for you is for you and God will always have the final say."

"Don't talk to me about God as mad as you have gotten at your mother for trying to teach all of you. You would rather not talk to your mother than to listen to her pray or tell you how God has continued to bless your family."

"Well, after the death of my sister, my mother questioned her faith too, so I can't be doing too bad by questioning him."

"What you say? You think it's okay to question God and the things he makes happen in our lives."

"This coming from somebody who just finished questioning God about their life. Fuck outta here trying to tell me what I should and shouldn't be doing."

Ariana stood from her seat. It was clear that she and Levi weren't going to get anywhere until she made a decision on what she wanted to do about the pregnancy and he was ready to sit down and decide on what he wanted to do about their relationship.

"I gotta do something. I'll get up with you sometime later."

"Yeah, I bet. What you bout to go see Amp? Do you even know he's in the hospital?" Hearing Ariana say that stopped time for Levi. He didn't understand why she would be telling him that. He knew that if something happened to Amp, someone would've called and told him.

"That's not funny, Ana. I understand that you don't like him, but for you to make up lies like that ain't cool at all," Levi barked.

"What reason would I have to lie on him? I don't know him like that he's never done anything personally to me. I wouldn't benefit from lying on him."

"You would benefit from lying on him. Telling me that he's in the hospital to keep me away from him so I could spend more time with you."

"Well, I'm sorry you feel that way, but that's not the case at all. If I have to lie to you to get you to stay with me, then I seriously don't want you or our relationship and the fact that you don't even trust me enough to believe me about what happened lets me know that this relationship has no trust at all and this really may never work."

Levi pondered over the news that Ariana had just given him as she stood before him scrolling through her phone. Ever since things went down between him and Zech, he hadn't left his room, wasn't answering the phone and wouldn't even open the door. That morning he thought his brother had come to his senses and was returning to their room to make things right between the two of them.

"Check this out," Ariana spoke, interrupting his thoughts as she handed him her phone. She'd gone to Amp's Facebook page where there were several posts with people wishing him well and asking him to get better soon. It didn't say exactly what happened to him, so that worried him more.

"Damnnnnn..." he blurted out as he scrambled through the room trying to find something to throw on, so he could get up to the hospital.

"See what I mean? Just like that, you're overlooking what's going on with me and your child to go run after some nigga that don't even really like you. Don't you think people know how he treats you like a flunky? Yeah, we all know. Like you his little bi-."

Levi chose not to respond to her. He continued getting himself prepared to go to the hospital to check on Amp. Not knowing what hospital he was in, and not wanting to ask Ariana, he figured he would call around to see if he could find out where he was.

"You know what... Screw you, Levi. And this damn baby that probably would've come out looking nappy headed like you. I don't want or need anything in my life that'll remind me of a good for nothing son of a b-." The look in Levi's eyes silenced her.

"This is my last time telling you to get out of here before you make me do something that I'm sure I WON'T regret." He made it a point to emphasize WON'T so that she'll know he had no problem messing her up.

Ariana ran out the door to get out of Levi's view. From experience, she knew what the wrath of Levi looked like, and she didn't want to be on the receiving end of it. Levi remained still as he watched her exit the room. He practically jogged to the door to lock it behind her, then turned to finish getting dressed. Bending down to lace his black Air Force ones, he paused to pull out his phone to call Zech. He knew Zech didn't care for Amp, but he still thought he should know that something was up and could lead to them being hurt too. Levi was determined to get to Amp and find out what had happened, so he'd know if he needed to watch his back or not. When Zech didn't answer, he headed out the door of the dorm and towards the front lobby. He called an Uber to take him to get his car from in front of Amp's house and prayed that when he got there, someone would be able to give him a little insight on what happened.

Chapter Thirteen:

Zechariah

The events of the night before were on repeat in Zech's mind. The fact that his brother practically turned his back on him for someone that wasn't as loyal as Levi believed was the most troubling of it all. He could deal with the betrayal by Amp and the way that they talked about him, but for him to go to his brother to try to reason with him and all his brother could do was shun him; that hurt him to the core.

Knowing that it wasn't a good idea for him to go back to the dorm, he checked into the Chicago Lake Shore Hotel. It wasn't too far away from the school which allowed him to remain in the area, near his brother, in case something popped off. Yeah, he was pissed at his brother, but that was still his blood, and he would die trying to protect him.

Zech sat at the foot of the bed and watched the video that he recorded from the night before. Hearing his is phone ring while he watched the video he saw it was Levi calling, but he was still too upset to talk to him right then, so he let it go to voicemail. Levi tried to call him back three more times, and each time Zech declined the call.

The phone rung once again, when Zech was about to decline it yet again, he saw that it was Mia calling. He was surprised because he knew he didn't give her his number, so how was she able to call him?

"Hello," he picked up by the time she hung up.

"Hey stranger. How are you?" His brows furred as he stared at the phone. He'd just saw her the night before, so what was with her calling him stranger.

"You just saw me, so how am I a stranger?"

"You'd think that after the way I put it on you, you'd been calling me first thing this morning."

"The way you put it on me? Naw, the way I put it on you. Get it right!"

"I'll give you that; you did a lil something," Mia laughed.

"A lil' something. Girl, I had you calling on God." They both laughed. "But, what's up girl? What you getting into today?"

"I'm waiting for my man to tell me what WE are doing," she offered.

"Oh, I didn't know you had a man. My bad for last night then. I promise not to tell anybody if you won't."

"Fool, I'm talking about you," she corrected him.

Zech was stunned by what she'd just said to him. All they did was share one passionate night that apparently, they both needed. How did she go from that to making him her man just that quick?

"You there?"

"Yeah, I'm here. I'm just trying to process what you said to me. We never discussed being a couple and I thought what we did last night was something to do between two consenting adults," he explained.

"Oh, well I didn't understand that. You like me, right?"

"Yeah..."

"And you're single, right?"

"Of course, I am."

"Then what's the problem? You were trying to talk to me the day I showed up at Amp's house. Were you only trying to get a sniff of what was between my legs?"

"I'm not even that type of guy. If I wanted to get down with you like that and not deal with you any longer, then we wouldn't be having this conversation right now. Remember, you put your number in my phone, so I could've easily curved you if I didn't want to be bothered with you," he explained.

"Uh huh, don't try to play me, Zech."

Zech was still unsure as to what she was talking about. He meant what he told her about trying to curve her. He'd been in situations where he didn't want to be around women, but he'd be nice enough to get their numbers and dip out on them. They quickly made the blocked list if he felt like they wouldn't be up to his standards. So far, Mia hadn't given him the impression that she'd be crazy or clingy, so he was willing to see how things would play out.

"Hellooooooo... Zech, are you listening?"

"Uh, yeah, I'm here. What you say?"

"If you were listening, then you would've known what I said," she nagged.

"Well, on that note... I'm going to go ahead and end this call. I don't do the naggin'. We can chill from time to time, but in this short conversation, I already caught that we wouldn't make it."

"First of all, I wasn't naggin you. I was simply stating facts that if you were listening to me, then you would've heard me when I said that I was only messing with you. I'm not trying to find a boyfriend. We can do the friends with benefits thing, but relationships ain't for me."

"Oh okay. That's cool with me. So, when we gonna get down again?" Zech joked.

"When I can find time in my busy schedule to deal with the lil something you be trying to do," she scolded and then hung the phone up on him without giving him the chance to respond.

Naturally, he called her back, which is what she wanted him to do. He felt like she was testing him to see just how interested he was in her and he obliged her.

"What?"

"Don't what me."

"I'm sorry, how may I help you?"

"Mia? You on some bullshit. Either you messin' with a nigga or you not. You not about to have your cake and eat it too."

"Fine. You can take me out later tonight," she insisted.

"I guess I can make that happen. It depends on how you act throughout the day."

"And how are you supposed to know how I'm going to act when you aren't going to be around me until tonight?"

"You better be sending me a text and checking in. That's the only way I'm going to know you serious about us. If I don't hear from you, then this relationship will be over before it starts." That was his turn to hang up on her.

Zech thought about calling Levi back to see if he'd heard what happened to Amp, but he didn't bother trying. He didn't feel like engaging in another argument with his brother about something neither of them could control. Zech watched the news to see if he'd see anything on there about Amp or Jaclyn, but he didn't. He considered driving by the house to see if the police even knew what had happened, but he didn't want to put himself in the line of fire. If someone were to see him, they could easily try to point him out as the person who killed them, and he wasn't trying to risk that. Instead, he decided just to lie down and wait for the time to pass so he'd see if Mia would indeed reach out to him throughout the day. That would determine if he did call her back and try to take her out on a date. Until then, he would continue to lay low in his room and at least try to catch up on some much-needed rest. He tossed and turned the entire time he tried to sleep the night before. Something didn't feel right to him, and he couldn't put his finger on it. Whatever it was, he knew it'd come to him sooner, rather than later, or so he hoped.

Chapter Fourteen:

Esther

Esther abruptly sat up in her bed. Beads of sweat invaded her forehead as her heart beat like it were about to jump out of her chest. She couldn't understand what was going on with her, but she sensed that something wasn't right.

"My boys," she rattled off as she searched her bed for her glasses. Once locating them, she threw the covers back and got out the bed. She scrambled through the house trying to remember where she'd left her cell phone.

"It has to be in here somewhere," she told herself while throwing couch pillows on the floor in the living room. She remembered being on the phone with her sister, Martha. She replayed the events of the night before in her mind to try to recall where she'd placed her phone.

Esther had just gotten home from a twelve-hour shift at the emergency room. She was a nurse, and her children did not know of it. Before they were born, she went to school to become a licensed practical nurse (LPN). As she was about to begin school to get her Bachelor of Science in Nursing (BSN), she found out that she was pregnant with

Ruth. Her parents weren't going to stand for watching another child, so she put the boys in childcare and worked to get a place of her own before Ruth made her grand entrance into the world.

Since she put off finishing school to care for children once they left for college, she started working back on her dreams. She decided to go to the local community college and finish out the registered nursing (RN) program. The day she graduated was one of the proudest moments of her life. She wished she could've shared it with her children, but they weren't answering the phone for her.

Esther knew that Ruth's death took a toll on them all, but she didn't think her sons would turn their back on her. They were all mad at God for not allowing Ruth to pull through the turmoil of that night, but she knew that He didn't make any mistakes. Maybe the reason for Ruth's demise was because Levi was so far gone that something needed to happen to bring him back to where he needed to be. Esther hated to think that way, but she didn't have any other explanation as to why so much trauma had come to her family.

Ring... Ring... Ring...

"Who the hell could that be? I just walked in the house good..." Esther talked to herself as she flopped down on the couch to grab her phone.

Esther worked at a facility for individuals with intellectual disabilities. They weren't supposed to have their phone with them because in the past, a lot of workers thought it was cool to record some of the patients to share amongst themselves for laughs. To avoid even accidentally taking her phone with her, Esther would always leave her phone at home on the side table in the living room.

"Hello," she finally answered the phone.

"Damn... It took you long enough," her sister, Martha, fussed through the phone. Esther rolled her eyes because she didn't check to see who it was before she answered. She knew her sister was long winded and there was a possibility that she would be on the phone for a long time.

"Hey to you too, Mar-Mar."

"Hey Esther. What have you been up to?"

"The same thing I'm up to every day. Going to work and coming home."

"You heard from them boys of yours?"

"Nope and I'm not going to call them either. They know where home is and they know where I am if they need me."

"And you're okay if your children only reach out to you if they need you?" Martha challenged.

"Let's not go there today, okay? I'm tired, and I'm not in the mood to argue with you or anybody else about the way I choose to handle my sons. Now, what did you call me for?"

"Whatever, Essie. You always shut people down when it comes to them heathens, but you better know that they gotta answer to God for everything they do."

"Don't we all. Now, if you don't want anything, I have to get my bath and get to bed; I have another twelve-hour shift tomorrow."

"Well, hold on. I called to tell you about how the pastor been stepping out on his wife."

"Whaaattttt?!? You lying."

"If I'm lying, I'm dying. I got all the tea."

"Well spill it. Let my cup runneth over as it said in the twenty-third of Psalms."

Martha did just that. She told Esther everything that she'd heard about the pastor at the church and the many indiscretions he was involved in. Her mouth dropped open and remained that way as she listened to her sister talk. They stayed on the phone for an hour.

The conversation ended with Esther promising to visit her sister within the next few weeks. It was only a thirty-minute drive to Pascagoula, so she wasn't too worried about traveling by herself. She got up from the couch and went to the kitchen to get herself a bottle of wine to place in the freezer and chill. Once she finished running her bath water, setting candles around the tub, and setting up her Pandora playlist, she was ready for this relaxing bath she needed after such a long day. Esther was more than ready to unwind, and a few chilled glasses of wine would surely do the trick.

From the time she finished preparing herself for her soak in the tub, poured herself a glass of wine, she couldn't remember where she placed her phone. Even replaying the events from the night before didn't help her and it started to frustrate her.

"Damn... Where could it be? I got off the phone with Mar-Mar and went to the refrigerator to get the wine out..." As she recounted everything that she did, she moved along with the steps. She was surprised when she opened the refrigerator and found her phone sitting on the top shelf.

Esther rejoiced to herself and then immediately dialed Zech's number. He'd always been her favorite because he was the easiest to raise and barely gave her problems. He didn't answer the phone, so she left a message for him to call her. She hung the phone up and said a prayer to herself before dialing Levi's number. Of course, he didn't answer as usual. She at least knew that Zech would call her back; she didn't count on Levi saying anything to her for another two months, even then, he'd call and act like he never got her missed call.

The feeling she had that something wasn't right kept playing on her. She didn't know what was happening or why, but she felt a storm brewing. Accessing the prayer room that she hadn't been to since the night Ruth died, she dropped to her knees and did the only thing that she could think to do. She prayed. She prayed for peace; for a better understanding of her life; and that God kept the only two children she had left, covered in His blood.

"God, I know that I haven't come to you in a while. Please charge it to my head, not my heart. I'm still struggling with how my daughter was taken from us in the blink of an eye. Well, I'm coming back to you now. I promise that I'll find my way back to you the way that I did years ago. But know that whenever I am fully back, everything about your WILL, will be done. Besides, it's never too late to get right with God, right? Keep my son's covered and protected with your blood. These and all things I ask in your name... Amen."

Esther rose to her feet and tried to reach out to her sons again. When she couldn't, she figured they were busy and that she'd hear from them eventually. Until then, she'd continue to work on getting back close to God and finding a way to keep loving her children from a distance without harboring any resentment towards them for abandoning her when she needed them the most.

Chapter Fifteen:

Mia

Standing in front of her tall door mirror, she admired the way her red strapless bodycon dressed hugged every curve on her body. She wasn't going anywhere special with Zech, but she still wanted to look her best. It'd been a while since she'd given any man her attention, so she was interested in seeing how things would go that night.

Mia initially asked him to pick her up in front of her dorm, but she didn't like people all in her business, so she told him she'd meet him at the restaurant. They were going to eat at the Salonica Restaurant. It was near the University. It served American and Greek food. Mia contemplated trying the place out but didn't want to get her hopes up. She'd never eaten Greek food before and wasn't interested in trying anything new by herself.

A knock on her room door caused her to jump. She was so lost in thought, worried about how the date would go, she didn't expect the knock.

"Yes?"

"Hey girl, it's Tasha. What are you doing?" Mia rolled her eyes wondering what the hell Tasha wanted. They hadn't spoken to each other since Tasha was caught trying to cheat off Mia and lied and told the professor that Mia willingly shared her answers. She wanted to beat the breaks off Tasha, but she didn't want to get expelled from school.

"Getting ready to go out, what's up?"

"You not gonna open the door for me? You must be going on a top-secret mission or something."

"Naw. I'm not trying to lose focus on what I'm doing. What you need?" Mia inquired before finally opening the door.

"Girl, did you hear what happened to Amp?"

"Amp who?"

"Jaclyn's lil boy toy."

"Nope. Where is she anyway?" Realizing she hadn't seen her roommate in a few days.

"That's what I came to tell you. Word on the street is that she was with Amp when somebody rushed in and shot them," Tasha dramatically explained.

"What the hell you mean somebody shot them? Are they okay?"

"I dunno. We don't even know if it's true or not, but we haven't seen her in a while. Have you?"

"Naw. I ain't seen her since the other day, but if it were true, don't you think I would've known that?"

"Yeah, I guess so. You'll let us know if you hear anything, right?"

"Yeah. For sure," Mia lied. She knew that Tasha was all about mess and drama and she was not about to be a part of it. *If Tasha was so interested in what happened to Jaclyn, then she needed to find out on her own,* Mia thought to herself.

"Thanks girl. Where you headed? Looks like you got a hot date."

"Naw, just going to hang out with a friend."

"Uh huh... I bet it is a friend," Tasha winked before licking her lips and rubbing her hands together.

"Not that type of friend, Tasha, and it certainly ain't a woman," Mia acknowledged. She wasn't for that lesbian action that Tasha always tried to throw her way.

"Dang... Why you say it like that? Don't nobody want you."

"Tasha, you been trying to get with me since I stepped foot on this campus and I have to constantly break it down to you that I don't want you. Nothing against you liking women, but I don't swing that way and you know it's not something that God agrees with."

"Says who? All y'all people walking around here talking about the Bible and how my sexual preference is going to send me to hell, but what about what y'all do? Lying, killing, stealing, cheating, and I'm sure you're latest... FORNICATING! No sinner is worse than the other, baby girl," Tasha beamed before placing a kiss on Mia's check and leaving the room before Mia could say anything to her.

"Bitch," Mia mumbled to herself before combing her hair down and using the curling irons to bump the ends. She wasn't pleased with the way her hair looked, but it'd have to do until her parents sent her the monthly allowance and she'd be able to go to the hair salon and get it done. Mia didn't dwell on the way her hair looked. She just tucked it behind her ear, threw a headband over the top and gathered her things to leave.

"I hope he isn't the type of man that likes to be punctual," she said to herself. Even though the restaurant was not far from the campus, she knew that she was still going to be at least five minutes late.

She worked double-time walking to her car and cranking up. She didn't bother with putting on her seatbelt since it was literally around the corner for her. She ran a few stop signs trying to compensate for some of the time that was wasted talking to Tasha.

Mia was disappointed in herself when she pulled up and saw Zech leaned up against his car. He held his wrist up and checked the time when he saw her. She hurried to get out the car and ran towards him. Reaching his personal space, she leaned in and kissed him on the check.

"Don't be trying to kiss me, thinking it'll make things better. You're late."

"I know. But, it's only by a few minutes."

"One or two minutes doesn't matter, you are still late. I'll get at you later lil momma cuz I like my women to be punctual."

"You can't be serious right now. You act like I kept you waiting for twenty minutes or longer. Shit, everyone gets a grace period," Mia snapped.

"Everyone, but the women I deal with. That says a lot about a person."

"What says a lot about a person?"

"If you can't be on time for a date, then that means you'll be late for other important events in my life."

"That is so not fair."

"I'm just playing," Zech cracked. "Chill out, Mia. It's not even that serious. I just pulled up myself," he laughed.

"Ugghhhh... You make me sick!!!" Mia ranted. Zech stood there and continued to laugh at her.

They walked into the restaurant hand and hand. Everyone turned their attention to them as they walked in.

"What's with all the stares?"

"Either they like what they see or seeing me with a woman is new to them," Zech shrugged. Playfully, Mia punched him in the arm.

"Did I tell you that you make me sick today?"

"Did I tell you that you look gorgeous today?"

"Don't be trying to get brownie points with me, big head," Mia teased.

They exchanged small, yet playful conversation while they stood in line and waited for a table. It wasn't long before they were seated and ordered appetizers.

"So, tell me why you're single," Zech spoke to break the silence between them once they sat down.

"Men play too many games. Not to mention, I was true to my Christianity for a while. It wasn't until I got to college, started hanging around the wrong people that I choose to tuck my Christianity away and let loose."

"Tell me about it. Life for me is so much different than it was in Alabama."

"Alabama? Oh Lord, don't tell me you're an undercover country bumpkin."

"I got your country bumpkin. And no, I'm not. I'm me, and if people don't like that, there are plenty of ways for them to see themselves out of my life."

"So, you big on church and God too?"

"Yes. Well, I was. Why you acting so surprised?"

"Because you don't find too many men that are open about those things. Young men at that."

"Let's not talk about this anymore. Let's talk about when I'ma get to get in those guts again."

"You are such a pervert," Mia blushed.

"My bad, I'll stop."

"Naw, you good. I kinda like it," she replied.

The rest of their dinner went by smoothly. Mia wanted to talk to Zech about what she heard about Amp and Jaclyn in case there was some truth to it, but she kept her mouth shut because she didn't want to ruin the good vibe they shared between each other. They parted ways that night making plans to see each other again soon.

Mia made it back to her dorm with a smile on her face. As she made her way to her room Tasha rushed her trying to confirm what she just heard.

"Mia, where have you been?"

"What is it Tasha? I already told you that I was going out on a date."

"Well, this is important. Jaclyn and Amp were shot for real."

"Okay, well then where are they and why hasn't it been on the news."

"I dunno, but there's more tea to spill."

Mia allowed Tasha to enter her room. She listened intently as Tasha filled her in on a series of events that occurred over the past few days and something that could potentially affect her. She didn't know who attacked Jaclyn and Amp or why, but she prayed that they didn't link her to them and come after her next.

Chapter Sixteen:

Zechariah

Zech felt he'd gotten closer to Mia over a short period of time. With Levi not talking to him at the moment, he knew that he'd need a new shoulder to lean on and Mia could be that person. Having an extra shoulder to lean on was something he craved since the death of his sister. He was in the hotel room he'd been staying in, preparing himself to surprise Mia. He figured he'd hang out with her as often as he could since him and Levi hadn't made up yet and he had no plans on doing so anytime soon.

Knock... Knock... Knock

Three soft knocks at the door alerted him that someone. Nobody knew where he was, he thought, so there was no reason anyone should be knocking on his door.

"It's me, open the door."

"Me, who?"

"Mia." Zech rushed towards the door, but took his time opening it. He wondered how she even knew where he was because he didn't recall letting her in on his location.

"Mia who?"

"Boy, quit playing with me. This is important," she fussed from the hallway. Sensing the urgency in her voice, Zech pulled the door open and pulled her inside quickly.

"What's the problem and how did you find me?"

"It's not that many places you could've gone. Besides, I called around until I was able to pay the receptionist to tell me whether you were here or not."

"Do what?"

"Naw, I'm just messing with you. I called Levi and told him it was important, so he told me what hotel you liked to take your thots to and now here I am," she confessed.

"Remind me to find another hotel after tonight. If he'll rat me out to you, there's no telling who else he'll tell where I am."

"That's what I came to talk to you about. I think you're in trouble."

"Why would I be in trouble?" he confusingly asked.

"Did you take something that didn't belong to you?"

"Naw, why?"

"Word on the street is when Amp and Jaclyn were attacked the night she died, someone saw you running from the backyard with some duffle bags.

"Looking for me for what? I ain't take shit from them."

"Not from them, but you took something from Amp that they were looking for."

Zech's palms became sweaty and the pace that his heart was beating, picked up. He couldn't understand how he'd been identified when he thought for sure that he'd been careful. He never even knew that Amp was still alive and wondered why his own brother wouldn't tell him that someone had been out looking for him. If anybody knew anything about what was going on in these streets, Levi knew everything. Too bad he wasn't able to see that his so-called homie set them up.

"Are you okay?" Mia asked when she noticed how tense Zech became.

"Have you ever done something that you regretted?"

"We all have."

"No, I mean have you ever done something that you wish you could've taken back? Like something you knew you shouldn't have done, but you did it anyways?"

"One time when I was five, I went into a gas station with my oldest sister because my mother wanted us to go get her a Diet Coke and some hot fries. After we'd walked to the store, my sister told me that momma only gave her enough money to get her drinks and chips and that we'd be able to get one candy bar. She wanted a Snicker, but I didn't; they were nasty to me. I told her that I didn't want that, she told me to stick something in my purse and try to go out the store. I did what she said, but when I got ready to leave, the cashier stopped me. She told me she saw me in the mirror that was in the corner of the store and that she wouldn't call the police if I left without taking the candy. I was scared out of my mind, but I gave her the candy and took off running home. When we got home, my mother asked where the stuff was that she sent us to the store to get. I told her that they were out," Mia paused a moment to laugh.

"What happened?" Zech quizzed as he took a seat on the couch in the room. Mia wasted no time sitting down next to him.

"Of course, she didn't believe me. So, she called up to the store and the woman told her that she caught me trying to steal. When I tried to tell her that my sister told me to do it, she didn't want to hear it. As soon as my daddy got home, he turned me upside down holding me by my right leg and beat me until the belt broke into two. Even that didn't stop him from the bruising he put on my body, but I bet I didn't steal anything else."

"Wow, I never took you for a thief," Zech laughed, trying to take his mind off the things that were bothering him.

"Trust me when I say I've never done it again and would never do it again. I've done my best to avoid doing some of the crazy things I could've done in life, but it gets hard at times. Especially when you're around a family that's always involved in things."

"How often do you pray?"

"Excuse me? How often do I pray? Do you even know what prayer is?"

"You must take me for a real thug or something? Hell, even thugs pray. But, my family grew up in the church. We were there seven days of the week."

"Lawwddddd... Ain't no way I could do that. I mean I love God and all, but I don't want to be in somebody's church every day of the week," Mia confessed.

"Girl, you crazy."

"Naw, I just wanted to make you laugh. But, for real, there is one thing that I did that I regret every single day of my life. It's been the worse decision I could've ever made."

"You wanna talk about it?"

"If you promise not to judge me."

"Why would I judge you? You know about my life of crime. There's no reason for me to judge you or anyone else for the decisions that you made in your life," he assured her.

Mia made herself even more comfortable next to Zech by lifting his arm up and wrapping it around her shoulder while she rested her head on his chest. To him, it was as if they were cuddling, which was something he wasn't used to. In his mind, if he didn't allow himself to start having catching feelings for anybody, he'd be able to save his heart from being hurt.

"You sure you not gonna judge me?" Mia asked again.

"I promise I'm not going to judge you," Zech confirmed as he placed a kiss on her forehead.

"A few years back, my mother got sick and sent me to live with her sister in Alabama. Her sister had five kids. They didn't like me. They felt my life was better than theirs. Jealous because I had a lot of nice things, I didn't have to worry if I was going to eat or not. They had to fight for everything. I can admit my cousins had it hard, really hard."

"Wait… Why didn't she send your sisters?" Zech interrupted.

"My sisters are older than me, so they weren't living with us at the time. It was me and my mother, and she didn't know if she was going to make it or not. She didn't trust my sisters to take care of me if she did die, they were still young themselves."

"Oh okay. My bad, you can continue."

"Like I was saying, none of her kids liked me and would do any and everything to make my life a living hell. I tried to tell my mother the things they were doing to me, but whenever she talked to her sister, she would get a different story, so my mother thought I was lying. Anyway, one day, my cousin came to me and asked me to help him do something for him. At first, I was uneasy at about it. I didn't know what he wanted me to do or what he wanted me to do it for when he had two sisters of his own that he could've asked." Tears formed in Mia's eyes as she talked. Each time a tear slid down her cheek, Zech would use his hand to wipe it away.

"It's going to be okay. I'm sure it can't be that bad."

"Yes, it is. Someone ended up dying because of me."

"You killed somebody?"

"No, but I might as well have pulled the trigger myself because if I never would've done what I did, the girl would've still been alive," Mia explained as she the tears came rolling down her cheeks uncontrollably.

"What did you do, Mia?"

"He told me that they would like me. He told me that they would stop picking on me if I did what he wanted. All

I wanted them to do was to love and accept me. Being that my mother was so sick, I didn't know how long I was going to be there. I didn't know if my mother was going to die and I end up stuck in a home with my cousins who didn't like me. I didn't want to be the hated child, I didn't want my cousins to hate me."

"What did you do, Mia?" Zech asked again.

"He asked me to knock on her door and say my name was Jessica. I never asked him who the girl was to him or why he wanted me to do it. I just did it. When she came to the door, my cousin pushed me out the way and shot her twice. I took off running without looking back. I learned by the news that night, that she died."

Zech's mind began working overtime. There was no way in hell Mia could be the same Jessica that knocked on their door that night asking for his sister and played a role in his sister's death. NO, NO WAY! There was no way that the world was that small that they would end up crossing paths again. NO IMPOSSIBLE. He didn't know what to think or what to feel. Not wanting to give away that Mia was more than likely involved in the death of his sister, he did his best to remain calm.

"This girl that you're talking about, what, what was her name?"

"Ruth, I think her name was Ruth. I didn't know her. I just know that she used to hang with my cousin's girlfriend."

"What's your cousin's name?"

"Jermaine. His name was Jermaine."

"What do you mean his name WAS Jermaine?"

"A few weeks after that Ruth girl was killed, so was my cousin. I'm not sure if someone linked the murders together or if they killed him because his involvement with dealing dope, but they shot him three times in the back of the head and he died immediately."

Zech wanted to feel sorry for what Mia said about her cousin, but he couldn't. All he wanted her to do was to confirm what happened with his sister and why they felt the need to kill her when she had nothing to do with the beef her cousin had with his girlfriend.

"So, let me get this straight... Your cousin told you to knock on someone's door you didn't know, told to ask for a someone named Ruth, and when they asked who you were, he told you to say the name Jessica? You didn't think to ask him what the reason was that he couldn't do it himself?"

"He told me they use to mess around, and she wasn't responding to him anymore. I should've known that was a lie. I knew that the girl was always with his girlfriend. I learned that she saw him kill his girlfriend and he needed to get rid of her so that she couldn't identify him when the police came around asking questions."

Zech saw the tears fall from Mia's eyes and the remorse in her face, but he didn't care. The rage inside of him would no longer allow him to sit and pretend to be concerned with the person who helped his sister be murdered. He pulled his phone from his back pocket and began going through it.

"Oh, my God. Please tell me you're not about to call the police on me," Mia worried.

"Naw. I'm about to show you something."

"Show me what?" As Mia was finishing up her question, Zech found what he was looking for in his phone.

"This..." He turned the phone so Mia could see what he was searching for. Her mouth dropped when she saw the picture of Ruth hugged up with Zech and Levi.

"You know her?"

"THAT WAS MY SISTER," Zech exclaimed as he rose to his feet. Mia jumped up. Fearful, not knowing what was to come. She opened her mouth to speak, but Zech tightly wrapped his hands around her throat, prepared to choke her until she was no longer breathing.

Mia wailed her arms around trying her best to get Zech to let her go. The more she fought against him, the tighter his grip became. Visions of seeing his sister answer the door only to take her last breath invaded his mind. He kept replaying the events of that night as if he were reliving it all over again. Mia's saving grace was Levi rushing into the room to stop Zech.

Chapter Seventeen:

Leviticus

"What the hell are you doing?" Levi asked his brother as he pulled his hands from around Mia's throat.

"She killed Ruth!"

"What?"

"She killed Ruth! She's the Jessica bitch that came to the door asking for Ruth so that her punk ass cousin could kill her. They didn't have to take her away from us. She didn't deserve to die. They took our baby sister away from us."

"She didn't kill her, Zech. Jermaine killed her," Levi expressed. Zech curiously looked over at his brother.

"How did you know?"

"I found out a few weeks after it happened, after what happened to Ruth. I handled his ass as soon as I found out," Levi admitted.

Zech stood in awe at the fact that his brother knew what happened to their sister and didn't let him in on it. All those years passed with him having hatred in his heart and wanting to avenge his sister's death, only for his brother to already have taken care of it.

"Why didn't you tell me?"

"You were really going through it. We all were. I knew how much you loved our little sister. I didn't think you would be able to handle knowing who killed her. I took it upon myself to take care of it." Levi explained, but Zech wasn't trying to hear him.

Furious, Zech stormed through the room picking up everything that belonged. He needed to get away from there. He needed to get away from Mia and Levi to him. With Mia telling him that someone was after him and it being so easy for both Levi and Mia to find him, he had to go.

"What are you doing here?" Zech stopped long enough to ask his brother whom he hadn't seen or spoken to in weeks.

"Mia told me that someone was after you. I don't know what's going on, but I'm not going to stand by and allow someone else to try to take away someone else that I love." That was the first time in a long time that Levi admitted to having love for anyone other than Ariana and their mother.

"I've got to get out of here," Zech scoffed.

"Tell me who's after you and why…"

"I can't get into all of that right now. I don't even know who's after me or if what she told me was true."

"It is true. I have no reason to lie to you. They are coming for the money, and they will kill you," Mia finally stated when she was able to regain control of her breathing. Instead of sticking around, she grabbed her purse and walked out the door. "I hope they kill you," she viciously spat.

"Bitch, I'll kill you," Zech replied as he charged her. When Mia saw him coming, she put a little more pep in her step and hightailed it out the room. Levi grabbed ahold of Zech before he could reach Mia.

"Calm down."

"Don't tell me to calm down. How can you be so calm about what she did? She was the one that knocked on the door, and her cousin was the one that killed her. She is responsible for our sister's death."

"I understand that I do, and I promise she's going to get what's coming to her, but you have got to move from here if someone is after you. What money is she talking about?"

"I can't get into all of that right now. Help me get my stuff so we can go," Zech ordered.

Normally, Levi would've stood his ground and argued with his brother, but he knew this wasn't the time. Once they were both in a safe location, that would be the time for them to have their talk.

"Where are you planning to go?"

"I dunno, but I know I need to get away from here." That's when it hit Levi, the best and safest place for him to go.

"You need to go home."

"Are you crazy? I'm not going back to that dorm. The campus security ain't worth a damn. I'll be dead before you could even dial 9 on your phone to call 9-1-1-."

"No, I meant go home-home. HOME as in where our mother is."

"I didn't think of that. But, I'm not sure if I'm ready to face ma yet. It's been three years since we last went there. She might not want me there."

"Zech, you've always been here favorite. If she wanted anybody there with her, it would be you. You just better be prepared to go back to going to church seven days a week," Levi chuckled, but his brother paid him no mind. "You got everything?"

"Yeah, hold this." Zech handed Levi the bags he initially started to carry before going to the closet and removing the two duffle bags that contained the money.

"Where the hell you get all this shit from? I only saw you take these two bags when you left the dorm."

"I went shopping, damn! Now, you gonna help me carry this stuff or no?"

"I got you. Let's go..."

The two brothers headed out the room being sure to give it one last look to check that they had everything before leaving out. Passing the front desk, Zech made sure to check out and get the remainder of the money back he paid for the week since he wasn't going to be staying there. Outside, they piled everything up in the back of

Zech's car and slid inside. Zech was in the driver's seat, and Levi was in the passenger seat.

"You gonna call her or you want me to?"

"I'll call since you think she likes me better," Zech laughed.

"You laughing, but we both know that's the truth."

"Whatever. I'll put it on speaker. We can call together," Zech suggested.

Levi shrugged instead of responding. He pondered over what their mother was going to say to them for not being in contact with regularly.

"Hello," their mother's sweet voice came over the phone. For some reason, a lone tear dropped from Zech's eye. Levi couldn't understand what it was, but he pushed his thoughts to the side and just chalked it up as the connection Zech, and their mother always had.

"Hey ma," Zech finally greeted her.

"Hey baby!" The excitement was evident in Esther's voice. "How have you been? I can't remember the last time I talked to you."

"I've been doing good. I'm sorry for not keeping in touch with you the way that I should, but I was wondering if I could come home and visit you for a while. I miss you." Levi thought Zech was laying it on strong, but truthfully, he did miss their mother.

"You're always welcome to come here. My home will always be your home. How's your brother?"

"I'm fine ma," Levi responded.

"Are you coming to see me too? I'd love to have both of my handsome boys at home. You can accompany me to church; the pastor and the rest of our church family have asked about you a lot." Levi turned his nose up at the thought of going to church, but if him going home was what it was going to take to buy him some time to find out what was up with his brother and to figure out to keep him alive, he was more than willing to do it.

"Yeah ma, I'll be there, too."

"I'm so excited. I can't wait to tell everybody that my boys are coming. When do you think you'll make it?"

"We should be there tomorrow afternoon," Levi informed her.

"Good. That means you'll be here in time to go to Bible Study."

"Now listen, ma. I'm not coming down there to be sitting up in chu-."

"That's fine, ma. We'll be glad to go with you," Zech interrupted Levi. They talked to their mother a few more minutes before hanging the phone up.

"Why you tell her that we'd be happy to go to Bible Study with her? I'm not going to visit her so that she can force church down our throats again."

"You know how much church means to her. I'm surprised to hear her say that she started going back. You know how she questioned her faith after what happened with Ruth. Let's see her how she always was to us and not steal her joy," Zech directed.

"If you say so, but if she tries to get me re-baptized or starts putting olive oil on my forehead talking about its holy oil, then I'm out." The boys laughed as they discussed their plans.

Zech cranked the car up and headed towards their dorm. Levi jumped out so that he could pack a few things for their trip. He didn't pack much because he didn't plan on being gone that long. While Zech waited for Levi to come back, he drove around the campus. He knew if someone spotted his car, they would be hot on his trail and he didn't need anyone following him; especially, with him going to his mother's house. There was no way he'd be able to forgive himself if he were to put her in danger.

Meanwhile, in the dorm, Levi grabbed two duffle bags and loaded them down with all the clothes he could. He hoped only to be gone a few days. Quickly grabbing what he needed, a sheet of paper was slid under the door. His heart rate increased as he wondered what was written on the paper.

Slowly he made his was to the door. Carefully he the door and stuck his head out to see if he'd be able to see someone walking away. But the hall was empty, no one in sight. He pulled his head back in and picked the note up. It read:

"I TOLD YOU FOOLS THAT YOU WERE GETTING INTO THE WRONG PROFESSION. YOU STOLE FROM ME, AND NOW I'M COMING TO GET WHAT'S MINE. WATCH YOUR BACK BECAUSE I'M KILLING EVERYTHING THAT'S KEEPING ME FROM WHAT'S RIGHTFULLY MINE. BANG... BANG..."

Whoever wrote the letter had the nerve to draw a gun at the end of it. Levi took it as it their signature and even more reason for him to take the note seriously. Levi urgently finished packing, grabbed the letter, and headed for the door. He reached downstairs and noticed that Zech was nowhere to be found. He wondered if Zech was the one that put the letter under the door to scare. To force him to not deal with Amp any longer.

Taking his cell phone out, Levi quickly dialed Zech's number. Zech didn't answer the phone which infuriated Levi.

"Where the hell this nigga at?" Levi asked aloud to no one in particular. That's when Zech came out of nowhere, blowing his horn. "Bout time," Levi mouthed as he made his way to the car. Wasting no time threw the bags the backseat and jumping into the passenger seat.

"You slow as hell."

"Shut up. I had to make sure I had everything!"

"You moved like you stuffed the whole damn room in your bag." Levi laughed at his brother's accusation.

"Whatever fool. I know what I needed. Plus, I didn't want to risk someone coming into the room and taking any of my electronics while we were away. If I could've grabbed the flat screen, I would've gotten it too." Zech just shook his head at his brother's revelation he laughed. "What you laughing at?"

"You. You a few slices short of a loaf."

"Well, that ain't nothing new," both brothers laughed.

Sitting in silence for another five minutes, Zech finally moved the car away from the school. They drove in silence with Levi's mind all over the place. He wanted so badly to make sure his brother was fine, but there was something he had to do before he left. If he didn't do it, he'd never be able to forgive himself.

Chapter Eighteen:

Ariana

Ariana sat in her living room balling her eyes out at the thought of being a single parent. She hollered out to Levi things that she didn't mean, and she didn't think she'd be able to express those things to him again because she knew she'd royally pissed him off.

Bam... Bam... Bam...

Bamming on her door startled her. She wasn't expecting anybody, and it was too late in the evening for missionaries to be coming to the front door. Ariana stood up to peek out the blinds, praying that whoever was on the other side didn't see here.

"I know you're in there. Open the door." She was shocked to see that it was Levi beating on her door like a crazed man. Ariana snatched the door open and hollered.

"What are you doing? You're going to make my neighbors call the police."

"I don't give a damn about that. I need you to pack and go somewhere with me."

"Are you crazy? I saw how angry you were with me the last time we talked. I'm not about to let you take me off somewhere and I don't wake up."

"Ariana? Really?"

"Yes, REALLY, fooling around with you, you never know," she solemnly responded.

"Listen, there's some stuff going down, and I need to get you and the baby away from here before someone comes after you. Please, trust me on this. We won't be gone for too long," he explained.

"And where exactly are we going?"

"We are going to see my mother," he exclaimed. "Your parents may not care for me, but my mother is nothing like that. She's a God-fearing woman. I'm sure she'll help us get a better understanding of our relationship and what we need to do about the baby."

Ariana was shocked at the stuff Levi was saying to her. She thought the last time that she saw him, it was the end of them for good. Now, he wants her to go meet his mother. That was a big step and one that she couldn't pass up.

"Fine, but if you try anything, I'm going to press charges."

"Trust me, Ana, if I wanted to do something to you, I wouldn't have come here. I've had plenty of opportunities to make you disappear, so don't flatter yourself."

Levi said what he needed to say and then he turned and left out the house. Ariana went to her room and grabbed as much stuff as she could think to grab to at least last her a week. She wished she knew how long they'd be gone.

Once she was packed, she walked through the house making sure to unplug the things that could be unplugged and making sure all the lights were off. She then grabbed all of her bags and marched towards the front door. Setting her alarm, she closed the door behind her and locked it.

"You could at least help me carry my bags; I'm pregnant remember?" Ariana hollered towards the car.

"Don't be trying to use that pregnancy excuse with me until I know for sure that I'm going to be a father," Levi snapped back.

"I'm not about to do this with you Levi and don't think for one minute that I'm about to get in front of your mother and clown with you."

"You better not get in front of my mother acting ratchet. That's one thing she didn't tolerate, and she'll have no problem putting you out of her house," he assured her. Zech never opened his mouth; he sat back and laughed at the way they interacted with each other.

Ariana stood outside the car for a good ten minutes waiting for someone to get out and help her. When they didn't, she let out a deep sigh and drug her bags behind her to the trunk. Zech hopped out the car to help her put everything inside and then motioned for her to go ahead and get in.

Zech jogged back to the front of the car and jumped in. It didn't take him long to put the car in reverse and zoom out of the driveway.

"Why are you going so fast?" Levi looked up from his phone to inquire.

"You don't see the car that was creeping up on us?"

Both Levi and Ariana turned their heads to see if they could identify the car. Neither of them had seen the car before, but it was clear that the car was following them.

"What's going on? What have you gotten me into, Levi?"

"I'm going to explain it to you when we get to my mother's house. Until then, you're just going to have to trust me."

"Trust you? Ain't no way I'm going to trust you when you came to my house after being distant with me for a few days and uprooted me, and now someone is following us. Is someone trying to kill you?"

"No, but they are trying to kill me," Zech stated.

"Kill you for what? What the hell is going on?" Ariana started spitting out whatever came to her mind, whether it was good or bad. Levi and Zech were in the front seat trying to come up with a plan to ditch the car following them.

"I know I told you I'd explain later. Sit back and quit asking all those questions," Levi directed and then refocused his attention on his brother and the unwanted car behind them. "What are we going to do?"

"Sit back... I got this." Zech remained calm and did his best to drive as normal as possible.

"Why you going so slow?"

"I don't want to let them know that we see them behind us." Levi nor Ariana understood Zech's logic, but they both sat back and put their seatbelts on. They both appeared to be scared which was unusual for Levi considering he always tried to act hard.

Getting away from the residential neighborhoods, Zech sped and kicked up rocks trying to get away from the car. Zech was sure the car behind them didn't expect him to take off the way that he did, so it was easy for him to lose him after hitting several corners and turning off in an alleyway. They remained parked behind a dumpster for ten minutes, allowing the car to travel around their vicinity to look for them. Figuring they'd gotten rid of them, Zech threw the car into reverse and backed out of the alley. He surveyed the area before pulling onto the street and heading towards the interstate.

"What you gonna do about gas?"

"We'll get it when we get a good distance away from here. I don't want to risk them catching back up to us." What he said made a lot of sense, so Levi didn't bother questioning him again.

Ariana sat in the backseat, scared out of her mind. *What have I gotten myself in*to, she thought while trying to figure out if being with Levi was worth all of this worth her possibly losing her life. She loved the fact that he didn't leave without her and wanted her to meet his mother. He'd never told her that before, so that made her fall in love with him all over again. She just prayed to herself that him telling her he wanted her to meet his mother was not another one of his ploys to make her keep the baby.

Chapter Nineteen:

Esther

"Yes, Pastor Flannery, both of my boys are on their way home," Esther excitedly told the pastor of her church.

"Does that mean you're willing to renew your faith and work on getting closer to God again?"

"I ain't say all that. All I know is that my sons are coming home, and I need to get them back into the church."

"You have to lead by example. How are you going to try to direct their walk into the right direction when you aren't walking in the right direction yourself."

"Pastor Flannery, I like you and everything, but don't come into my house and trying to tell me how to live. I know all about God and how he allowed some hoodlum to step foot in my apartment and kill my one and only daughter," Esther ranted.

"No need to get so heated, Sister Esther. Everything happens for a reason, and in due time, you'll understand what the reasoning was behind the death of your daughter."

"You don't even believe that shit yourself. Look at you... You sitting in front of me looking like a hypocrite. You walk in that pulpit every Sunday trying to tell people how to change their lives and how to live right, but are you?" she challenged.

"Am I doing what? Living right? Of course, I am."

"Cut the bullshit. We all know you sleeping with Sister Blanchard. We got the screenshots of all the conversations between her and a copy of your lil fellow down there," Esther pointed and chuckled. She laughed because the pastor was very handsome, looking at him, one would think was working with something. However, by the picture sent out showed he was no bigger than her pinky finger. Esther was in such a good mood before the Pastor came, but now he was pushing his luck with her, she had no problem calling him out on it.

"I'm shocked. Never in a million years would I expect this behavior from you. Whatever you think you've seen between Sister Blanchard and me is not true. I can also assure you that whatever picture you have was not an actual part of my body," he tried his best to assure her, but she wasn't trying to hear it. She'd already made up in her mind that he wasn't living right and really didn't have the right to tell anyone else how to live their life.

"If you say so, Pastor. Besides, who am I to judge? That's why I stay my senior citizen ass at home. What you do with your body and what's between your legs is your business, you'll have to answer to God for any wrongdoings you've done or are doing."

"This isn't getting anywhere and I'm not bout to sit here and let you talk to me like you're the pastor and I'm a basic church member."

"Oh, so you're saying that if we aren't pastors, then we are only basic people? Did I hear that correctly?"

"Every time I say something to you or let you know what's going on, you're blowing it making it something bigger than what it was. I'm not about to play with you, Pastor."

"Esther, I can tell that something is really bothering you. I'm not about to argue with any of my church members. IF you get to a point that you want to talk to me about something, GOD Related," he emphasized, "then we will have something to discuss. Until then, you have a blessed day." With that, the pastor hung the phone up. Esther laughed at herself and how'd she'd been able to get until his skin. Excited about her sons coming home, she decided to call her sister, Martha, and let her in on the information.

"What?" Martha answered with an attitude.

"Dang girl, what's wrong with you?"

"Oh, I'm sorry, sis. I thought you were one of these bill collectors. They keep calling me about what I owe and what Ronnie owes. Hell, they should know if I can't pay them what I owe, I'm not about to come out of pocket to cover someone else's bill."

"You need a new number or better yet, a new man."

"Ha-Ha… Heifer, you not funny."

"Who said anything trying to be funny? What has Ronni been able to do for you since you've been together? I'll wait…". The phone line grew silent because neither woman had a thing to say. Esther wasn't trying to make fun of her sister's relationship or bring her down; she wanted her sister to see that there was more to life than the misery she received from her dead-end relationship.

"I gotta go," Martha finally spoke. Esther knew that was coming that's what always happened whenever anybody tried to get Martha to see the error of her ways.

"Wait... Before you go, I have some good news for you.

"If ain't nobody hit the lottery or got no money to give me, then there ain't nothing good that you can tell me."

"My boys are coming home. They are coming to visit me for a while."

"What's so good about that?"

Esther couldn't believe the response Martha had given her about such great news. Everyone knew how she felt about her boys and how them turning away from her and God after Ruth's death caused her to slip into depression. She hoped that someone would be happy for her. However, it wasn't looking that way.

"Nothing. I'll talk to you later," Esther snapped and then hung the phone up. She wasn't about to tolerate no disrespect or listen to anyone degrade her relationship with her sons. She'd watch them burn in hell before that happened.

Esther walked towards the bedroom that once belonged to Ruth. Most people would've moved out of the house their child was killed in, but not her. She had too many memories there and wanted to remember all of the good things she could. She hadn't touched a single thing in Ruth's or the boy's room since they were all gone. She thought about opening Ruth's door but decided against it. Instead, Esther opened the door to the boy's old room. She set her mind on getting the room together for their visit because no matter what anyone had to say about them, they were still her children and she would love them despite their differences.

Chapter Twenty:

Mia

After revealing to Zech that someone was after him, Mia had been trying to lay low. She heard that both brothers skipped town, so she knew it would be a matter of time before someone came after her for giving them a heads up. She wondered if they'd be able to link things back to her telling them, but she knew they'd never believe someone else told them.

Mia had been sitting in her dorm for over a week. It was Wednesday, and the semester ended on Friday. She felt if she could make it through the last two days of class and leave campus heading back home Saturday, she would be safe.

Ring… Ring… Ring…

Mia rolled over in her bed to the sound of her phone ringing. She didn't know who'd be calling her so early in the morning, so she pressed the button to send it to voicemail. She figured they'd leave a message if they really wanted to talk to her.

Silencing her phone, she rolled back over and looked towards the window. The blinds were closed, so she didn't know what the weather looked like outside, she hoped it'd be a beautiful day. Thoughts of Zech plagued her mind. She couldn't stop thinking about their many lovemaking sessions. It hurt her to her core when Zech revealed to her she was partially to blame for the death of his sister Ruth.

Ring... Ring... Ring...

Mia's phone began to ring again, annoying her. This time, she retrieved it from under her pillow and checked to see who was calling. She didn't recognize the number, but she answered anyway.

"Hello," she softly spoke.

"Bitcccchhhhhh... Wake up!" It took her a minute, but she was able to recognize that it was her friend, Celeste.

"Why are you calling me from a different number?"

"Because when I just tried to call you from my number, you slick sent me to voicemail. I know you didn't think I wouldn't catch that." Mia began to laugh.

"My bad girl, I'm a little tired. What have you been up to?"

"Nothing. Just trying to prepare for the last of my finals, then back home for summer break. What about you?"

"The same,' Mia responded with some hesitation. Her mind was all over the place. She grew to like Zech but figured that her revelation would prevent them from being anything to each other.

"He acts like I knew that was his sister," she spoke loudly to herself.

"What are you talking about, girl?" Celeste's voice helped her to realize that she had spoken out loud.

"Oh, nothing. I was talking to myself."

"I know and to be honest, I was waiting for your ass to respond to yourself. I would've been on the first thing smoking trying to figure out how to get a check for you," Celeste cracked.

"Whatever. What do you want anyway? It's too early in the morning for any foolishness."

"Too early in the morning? Girl, it's two o'clock in the afternoon. What the hell you been up to that has your time messed up?"

"Just had a lot on my mind lately. You wanna get out and do something?"

"Yeah, let's go to the park

and walk around the track," Celeste suggested.

"That's cool. I'll come, let me go handle some business first and I'll catch up with you later."

"Aight. Just hit me back when you know what time you think you'll be able to make it."

"Okay girl, talk to you soon." The call ended, and Mia jumped out the bed and hightailed it to the bathroom. She'd been holding her pee for the longest and knew that she wouldn't be able to hold it for too much longer.

She knew she told Celeste she had some business to take care of, but she didn't. She just hated when people caught her off guard and asked her to do stuff with them. She'd feel obligated to say yes. She didn't even want to go walking with Celeste but said she would go because she didn't want to hurt her feelings by not going with her.

Mia knew it'd be a matter of time before Celeste called her back to see where she was and what time she planned on meeting her. Mia knew she didn't want to talk to her, so she blocked the number Celeste called from.

"With her aggravating ass..." Managed to get out before she heard a knock at her door.

Knock… Knock… Knock…

"What do you want, Tasha?" she chirped.

"I need to see if you got a pack of noodles I can borrow until my mom sends me some more money."

Mia went to open the door. She didn't like Tasha to come her for anything. Tasha was messy, and she wouldn't stop making advances towards Mia. Mia wanted to be left alone, but no one seemed to get it today.

"Look, I told yo-."

Before Mia was able to finish her sentence, she was met by a fist to the mouth. Then a punch to the face causing her to become dizzy, she stumbled back allowing her attacker to enter the room. Once inside Mia was punched in the face again, and again causing her head to snap back from the powerful punch. Falling to her knees unable to defend herself Mia was kicked and dragged across the dorm room floor. Her attacker yelled obscenities at her, all Mia could do was scream and wonder why no one was coming to her aid. With one final kick, Mia's eyes rolled to be the back of her head as everything began to turn dark.

Please cover me God. Don't let me die, she thought to herself as her eyes finally closed.

Chapter Twenty-One:

Ariana

"Levi, did you have to bring her?"

"Hell yeah. I'm not about to dip out, not knowing how long we gonna be gone and she think I abandoned her. I love her crazy ass and I don't want her to do anything drastic," Levi admitted.

"Drastic? What you mean?" Zech's eyebrow raised as he pondered what his brother could've been talking about.

"You remember me telling you that she was pregnant?"

"Yeah... And?"

"And, she talking about she doesn't know if she wants to have the baby or not. She thinks my involvement with Amp was gonna keep me running the streets and she'd be a single mother."

"Well, is there any truth to it? You know how bad ma it had raising the three of us alone."

"Come on, Zech. You know the type of man I am. I may not have listened to all that mumble jumble ma used to always say about being close to God, but I know how to be a good man. I've never skipped out on my responsibility;

thus, the reason I'm still in class no matter how late we stay out or what I've done before going. I ain't never cheated on Ariana, and I really can't see myself with anyone besides her. She's my heart."

"I'm proud of you, bro. I do know the kind of man you are, but you need to let her see first-hand how good you are. The reason I say that is because everyone else around you can see you as an angel and that wouldn't matter to her. It's about how she sees you in her eyes. Remember that," Zech preached and Levi soaked in everything that he said.

Ariana sat in the back seat with her head tilted to the side, listening to the conversation between the brothers. She wanted to say something to Zech about worrying why Levi picked her up to go with them, but she didn't. She didn't want them to know that she'd been eavesdropping. She wanted to hear the conversation play out.

"You know what you should do?"

"What's that?'

"You need to put Ma on her," Zech suggested.

"For what?"

"You know by the time ma gets done talking to her, I bet the only thing she'll be aborting is her thoughts about getting rid of the baby," both boys laughed.

"I can't stand you."

"But what I do? I'm giving you facts. You know ma not about to play with you, her, or nobody else."

"That is true. But, I'm not going to ever let it be said later on down the road that I pressured her into doing anything that she didn't want to do."

"I feel ya. Just make sure y'all sit down and talk about everything before either of you make a decision. I know you love her, but are you still going to be able to love her if she decides she doesn't want to have the baby?"

For a moment, there was nothing but silence in the car. Ariana thought it was because Levi was thinking about how he was going to respond to his brother's question. She kept her eyes closed because she was interested in what his response would be. She loved him true enough, but she knew she had to learn to love herself more than she loved anyone else.

"Look, if she gets rid of my seed, then I'm going to have to get rid of her," Levi chided.

"What you mean you gonna get rid of her?"

"I mean her family gonna be like Mary Mack, "all dressed in black" and there is certainly going to be some slow sanging and casket slanging."

"Bruhhhhh... Not Mary Mack..." Zech fell over the steering wheel laughing at his brother. Levi was off the chain at times, but the seriousness in his tone showed he wasn't playing. That somewhat put fear in Ariana. She didn't know that Levi had it in him to kill anybody and she didn't want to be the first one her family learned that he killed.

"I'm dead ass. She can play with me if she wants. I'll shake her ass up like a rag doll."

"I can't with you. I don't even see how you deal with that loud ass snoring she doing. She needs to be out there hibernating with bears or something, the way she sounds."

It took me a minute, but I got used to it. I remember the first few nights I stayed with her, I wanted to suffocate her. I put the pillow over her face and started pressing down on it. You should've seen how fast she woke up swinging her arms around like she was swimming, trying to get me to let her go," Levi cracked.

"What happened?"

"She woke up and started screaming, so I moved my hand and played like I was sleep. When she finally sat up and started panicking, I told her she was only having a dream. Mannnnn... the look on her face was priceless."

Ariana's eyes shot open and she opened her mouth to speak. She was stunned to see that they were parked in a driveway and both boys were staring back at her.

"Got yo ass. Stop trying to listen in to what we are saying," Levi smirked.

"You make me sick. How are you gonna try to kill me in my sleep?"

"How you gonna be disrespectful and interrupt my sleep by snoring so loud." Ariana stared at him for a few minutes, then rolled her eyes.

"Where are we?" she asked with a disgusted look on her face.

"This is our mother's place. Don't trip because you've seen worse. Now, I'm warning you my mother doesn't play. She's a Christian, but she is still a BLACK WOMAN and will break you down if she has to."

"I'm not worried about your mother, I know how to be respectful."

"I hope so because she can see through bullshit, too," Zech chimed in.

"Ain't nobody asked you nothing, and I have no reason to try to get over on your mother. Watch me work," she boasted before stepping foot out the car.

The brothers looked at each other and shrugged before they got out behind her. Zech blew the horn as he stood next to the car. He did it three times because that was always the signal they gave their mother growing up, letting her know that they'd made it home.

Esther came rushing outside to greet her boys. Ariana was closest to the door, standing there with her arms outstretched, prepared to receive Esther, but she ran right passed her and to Levi. While she hugged Levi, Zech came around the car and joined in on the hug. Ariana was embarrassed, so she put her hands down to her side. She was sure to look around and prayed that nobody saw what happened.

"Oh my... You look sooooo good," Esther cried. It was such a touching moment for them all. The boys tried to fight back their tears, but feeling their mother's nurturing embrace, broke them down. All three stood in the same spot for at least five minutes reacquainting themselves with each other.

"I missed ya'll so much. Don't ever run away from me like that again," Esther fussed before using her hands to swat at both boys.

"We won't," they said in unison.

"Ahem..." Ariana remained in her same spot as well. Only she was tapping one of her feet on the ground with her arms crossed over her chest.

"Oh, I'm sorry, Suga. I don't feed the homeless anymore. You have to go down to the church a few blocks away. It's called Mountain Dew Me Church of the Nazarene." The brothers were killing themselves laughing at what their mother just said.

"Ma, this is my girlfriend, Ariana."

"Do what? Son, I know you haven't been home in a while, but I know I told ya'll to never pick up strays."

"She's not a stray, Ma. She looks like that because I picked her up at the last minute to get her to ride with us.

We've been in the car all night and haven't had the chance to handle our hygiene."

"Oh, well I don't like her. Get rid of her and then come on in the house."

Zech and Levi looked at each other. They'd never seen their mother turn anyone away or pass judgment on them before getting a chance to get to know them.

"Give me a minute to talk to her," Zech told Levi and Ariana.

"Naw. We gonna go. Let me get the keys so we can go check into a hotel. We'll be back later to talk to her."

"No, you know I'm not about to let you leave me stranded and here with her by myself. Wait out her until I can talk to her and then we'll go from there."

"Aight. But you don't have long. Fix this or we're leaving. They are my family now, and momma can't disrespect them not in front of me I won't allow it," Levi expressed.

Zech told them okay and walked inside the house in search of their mother. Ariana didn't know how to take their mother not liking her without giving her a chance.

She couldn't figure out how she and Levi were both in families with a bunch of crazy relatives. Knowing there was nothing left for her to do, she went and sat back down in the car. She figured if she was going to have to play the waiting game, the least she could do was get comfortable while she waited.

Chapter Twenty-Two:

Zechariah

Inside the house, Zech followed the scent collard greens and ham hocks to the kitchen. He knew if his mother was cooking, there was no way she'd be gone too long away from her kitchen. She wouldn't even go to the bathroom without putting the food on simmer because she was afraid that she'd end up burning something.

"Hey ma," Zech walked in to find his mother sitting at the table.

"I was wondering when someone was going to come in and join me."

"We were coming, but I need you to reconsider the way you're feeling about Levi's girlfriend. He loves her."

"And? Why should I consider someone else's feelings when neither of you thought about mine when you walked out the door without looking back?"

"Ma, you know why we did what we did. It's not that we don't love you, but we had to get away from here. Both of us had so much hatred built in our hearts that we didn't want that to break us down. I'll admit we were wrong for not maintaining contact with you the way that we should have and I promise you that'll change."

"How do I know that?"

"Look at me, ma. I'm our son. You love me and know that I wouldn't lie to you." Zech was truthful in that. His mother never had to worry about him lying to her or trying to deceive her.

"How far along is she?"

"Who? How far along is who?"

"That girl out there saying that she's my baby's woman. She's pregnant. I can tell by how wide her nose is and that little bulge under her shirt." Zech's mouth dropped open as he listened to his mother tell him all the things that gave away the fact that Ariana was pregnant.

"Just let him be the one to tell you."

"Why?"

"Come on, ma. I don't want them thinking I came in her to gossip about them or something. Besides, it's not my business to tell. That's their news, and they have the right to tell you; not me."

"Do you have someone you want to bring in for me to meet, too?" His mother asking him that made him instantly think about Mia. He liked her and wanted them to be together somewhere down the line, but the way she played a part in his sister's death was nothing that he could look past.

"No ma'am. I've been focusing solely on school. I don't need nothing distracting me at the moment."

"You say that now, but there is some sadness in your voice as I listen to you speak. What happened between you and her?"

"Between me and who? I don't have a woman."

"You may not have one at this very moment, but there is someone in your life that has your interest."

"Naw. I've been staying focused on school. Besides, this is not about me. This is about Levi, Ariana, and their unborn child. I know you wouldn't turn away from your grandchild or son."

In the midst of Zech speaking to his mother, he kept hearing a whining sound. He looked around the room to see if maybe there was a television on or someone else there because he couldn't understand why he'd be hearing such a noise.

"What's wrong with you?"

"Do you have a pet or somebody here?"

"Oh, yeah. I need to introduce you to your sister."

"Sister?" Zech backed away from his mother. He stared at her as if he were looking at a double headed dragon.

Esther moved away from the kitchen and walked down the hall when she returned, she was carrying a toy long haired Chihuahua. The puppy yipped the moment she saw Zech standing there. Esther didn't have company often, so the puppy was excited to see someone other than her. Esther got closer to Zech, and the puppy instantly jumped out of Esther's arms, into Zech's. They both laughed at how happy both Zech and the puppy were.

"What's his name?"

"Her name is Judith."

"Really ma?"

"What? All my siblings have names from the Bible, and so do mine. Just because she's not a real person, doesn't mean that she couldn't receive a Biblical name." Zech shook his head because he knew how serious his mother was about what she said.

"Okay... But, enough about Judith. Are you ready to properly meet Levi's girlfriend?"

"Nope."

"Come on, ma. What would Jesus do?"

"He'd knock both of you upside your damn head for abandoning your mother the way you both did. The first time you two home, you bring along a straggler. I want to spend time with the two of you, and now not only does your brother bring his girlfriend, but she's pregnant."

Knock... Knock... Knock....

Esther's face balled up at the sound of someone knocking on the door. Zech knew that Levi wouldn't have been knocking, so he looked at his mother in a state of confusion.

"What did you do?"

"What do you mean? I ain't did nothing," Esther tried to play innocent.

"You really expect me to believe that? Any time you make that facial expression, I know something is up with you, so let's try this again... What did you do?"

Knock... Knock... Knock...

Someone was knocking on the door again, but instead of the person waiting for someone to come to the door, they pushed it on open.

"Esther, where you at in here? I saw my baby, Levi, outside; now, where is my boo, Zech?" The sound of his aunt, Martha's voice could be heard loud and clear. Zech hated being around her because she always tried to make her family seem better than anyone else's and they all knew that her husband liked to touch on small children. She was in denial about it. Esther wouldn't send her children to their home and if they saw their aunt, she'd have to come to their home alone.

"Hey Aunt Martha," Zech greeted her, trying to appear happy about seeing her. Martha knew how her family felt about her husband, so she never pushed the issue about him coming around. Seeing her nephews today for the first time in years had her emotional, but put a huge smile on her face.

Zech spoke to Aunt Martha while a bunch of other church members came pilling into the house carrying different dishes of food. The food smelled delicious, and Zech couldn't wait to dive in. His stomach growled thinking about the last time he had a home-cooked meal.

"I'll be right back," he told his mother as he went outside to get Levi and Ariana. Zech practically jogged to the car to get his brother.

"What took you so long and what's the problem?"

"She was upset because she wanted us to spend a few days with her alone since we hadn't seen her in a while. I guess she thought Ariana would serve as a distraction and keep you from being around her."

"Wow, I never thought about it like that."

"Me either, but luckily these people from the church showed up, so this is a good way to ease Ariana in."

"Hold up… How she gonna say she wanted a few days with us alone and she got all these folks in here?"

"Who you asking? But, you know when they leave, I'm going to tell her about the way she acted, only for her to turn around and do this," Zech announced.

"Good, somebody needs to get in her ass. Come on, baby. Let's go in here so you can get a feel of what down south food tastes like." Although hesitant, Ariana took Levi's hand and followed him back inside.

Zech stayed behind to gather their bags out the car. He mainly made sure to get the two large duffle bags he had with the money before he locked his car up. He wasn't crazy enough to leave something that important behind. He hurried to the front porch to go put the bags away in Ruth's old room. Nobody had been in there for a while and he knew it'd be the last place somebody would think to check for the money. Well, somebody that was familiar with the family because they knew that particular room was off limits. After depositing the money in the room, Zech said a small prayer to himself hoping that the little party his mother called herself surprising them with would go off without any further problems before he exited the room to rejoin his family.

Chapter Twenty-Three:

Leviticus

The whole time they were in Esther's house trying to fellowship with some of their old church members, Levi didn't feel comfortable about being there. The way she acted towards Ariana had him thirty-eight hot. He'd never seen that side of her before and wondered where it was coming from. How could she tell Zech that she was upset that they didn't spend time with her when she already had a get together planned? That didn't make any sense to him.

"I'm tired..." Ariana expressed as she groggily walked towards Levi.

"I can tell, too. Let me get Zech to take us to get a rental car and then we'll find a hotel to check into."

"Will your mother be mad if we don't stay here?"

"Where would we sleep? Zech and I shared a room until we left, and we had twin size beds and there is no way I'm going into Ruth's room," he asserted.

"That's fine. I'll go sit on the porch and wait for you."

"Okay. I won't take too long." Levi kissed her forehead and watched as she exited the house.

Levi moved over to the living room to a corner by himself. Removing his phone from his back pocket, he went to the website for Enterprise and reserved a car for that afternoon. He figured Zech probably wasn't ready to leave yet, so he wasn't going to bother him. The driver was scheduled to pick them up in thirty minutes, so he went in search of his mother to let her know that he was getting ready to go.

"Ma, let me talk to you," he told her as he wrapped his arm around hers and pulled her towards her bedroom.

"Finally, you have something to say to me?" Esther turned her nose up at Levi.

"Don't start with me. You know you were wrong for the way you treated my girlfriend."

"And you were wrong for bringing her here without consulting me. When do I get to spend some quality time with my children without other people being around?"

"There was a better way that you could've handled this entire situation, but you chose not to. I'm not about to play with you or anybody else when it comes down to the woman that I love. Now Ma, I love you too, but it's time for me to start my own family and that means you're going to have to respect the woman I choose to be with."

"I understand that, but still…"

"There is no but. She never disrespected you at all. All she wanted was to get to know her possible future mother-in-law, but the way you acted is a way that I'm sure is going to have her ready to flee from me when we make it back to school."

"I'm sorry. I know I was wrong, and I promise I'll apologize to her about it."

"It's cool. You can do it some other time. We're about to head out to get some rest. I'll be back over here first thing in the morning.

"Wait… you're not staying here? I have the room all fixed up for you and your brother."

"Ma, I have my girlfriend with me. Ain't no way I'm sleeping in a twin bed with her."

"Well, I'm sure you're sleeping in a twin bed with her on that campus because that's all they have in those rooms.

Plus, she's pregnant and there's no denying that you were doing something in that twin bed."

"I'm going to kill him," Levi fumed.

"Kill who?"

"I'm going to kill Zech. He had no business telling you about my situation."

"He actually didn't tell me anything. I can look at her and tell that she's pregnant. That little gut she has doesn't even fit her body and that glow to her explains it all. You may try to hide the pregnancy from other people, but you won't be able to get anything past your mother. I've been pregnant three times, so I know when someone else is pregnant." Levi thought long and hard about what his mother said to him and it made a lot of sense. Her clearing that up for him made him not want to hurt Zech anymore.

"I'll be back in the morning, Ma." Levi leaned in and showered his mother's face with kisses. Esther ate every minute of it up.

Levi left his mother standing in her room and went outside to get Ariana. By the time he got out the door, a car he'd never seen before pulled up in front of the house.

They must've came early, Levi thought to himself as he prepared to help Ariana off the porch. Levi glanced up again to take a better look at the car and it was as if a lightbulb went off in his head because he threw Ariana to the ground and yelled, "Get downnnnnnn..." hoping that the people inside the house heard him.

RATATATATATAT.... RATATATATATATATAT....

A series of gunshots rang out and the people inside of Esther's house scattered like roaches when a light was turned on. The crazy part about the entire scenario is that some of them ran outside while the gunshots were erupting, instead of getting down on the floor where they were on the inside. That was way better than running out the door.

The shooting went on for at least fifteen minutes, which was sad because not a single police officer showed up during that time. As soon as the shooting stopped, Esther ran outside frantic at what had taken place.

"My baby.... Nooooo not my baby. Don't do this to me again, God. I can't stand losing another child. Someone call the police, they shot my baby."

Everyone looked around to see what Esther was hollering about. None of it made sense because nobody had even had the chance to assess the situation or the scene yet.

"Please help me... God you told me that if I followed you, you would see me through. You said you would never but more on me than I could bear. I pray constantly, I believe in you, I live my life according to the Bible.... Why are you doing this to me?   Why can't you hear my prayers?" Esther stood in the yard with her arms outstretched, as she yelled up to the sky. Her yelling didn't last long at all.

RATATATATATAT.... RATATATATATATATAT....

The gunshots picked up again and lit Esther up like a Christmas tree. Instantly, she fell to the ground with her body continuously convulsing.

(To Be Continued...)

Made in the USA
Middletown, DE
13 October 2021